TOXIC DISTORTIONS

∽

Teddy Goldstein

Copyright © 2010 Teddy Goldstein
All rights reserved.

ISBN: 1456336681
ISBN-13: 9781456336684

For all families torn apart by suffering

DISCLAIMER

Although this book was inspired by the accounts of Holocaust Survivors like Marcel Ladenheim, and informed by a number of unassailable historical facts, gleaned from rigorous research, it is nevertheless a work of fiction. There are occasional references to real people and events from history, but these are simply intended to add to the authentic nature of the narrative. The names have been carefully chosen not to offend the living. The novel is a figment of the author's imagination. No more. No less.

Teddy Goldstein, January 2011

BOOK CLUB DISCUSSION POINTS

Please see the final pages of the book for this section.

Note: This book contains sexually explicit material.

PART 1

CHAPTER 1
London, 10 August 1965

No premonition. Narrow hall, serene in the early morning. Pastels seeping through fake Victorian glass. Door locked and chained. Barbour, umbrella, Hush Puppies and running shoes in their appointed places. The usual Guardian and a few letters litter the floor. Eyes blurred with waxy sleep, he scoops up the debris and takes it to the breakfast table. Swiss muesli, Cox's apple and rapidly cooling cup of tea. He glances idly at the paper, the editorial, words of sense in this anarchy. Now the post. Gas bill, junk mail. Then he sees it. Sad, grey envelope, Swiss stamp. He opens the envelope with one precise incision and removes the letter. Strange anachronistic, governmental motif, facing eagles glaring anxiously at one another above the photocopied text. Two smaller sheets – misty copies of old photographs.

Andreas Federiz, Avocat
Geneve
Confederation Helvetique
Telephone: Geneve 777342190888

5th August 1965
Dear Sir
Re: Michael Turner,

Toxic Distortions

We are seeking an individual who was born in early 1939. I enclose two photographs. One was taken in the early days of 1942 of a child whose name was Michel at the age of three, with a girl of a similar age. The other is an image of the boy's mother, a 25 year old lady whose name was Augustine Rosenberg and her sister Mathilde Auslander who was then 17.

If you recognise any of the people in these photograph copies, please can I know because I have something urgent and very important to communicate to the male child who will be an adult man by now.

*Yours faithfully,
Federiz, Andreas*

He fumbles with the photocopied images. First sheet, a chirpy three year old boy with long blond tousled hair, almost plump in patterned romper suit, grinning broadly at a new toy car, awkwardly holding hands with a skinny little girl, grumpy in a white dress which contrasts with the curtained background, a big bow in her skimpy hair, a foot thrust forward, a thin arm held up as if to ward off a blow from the photographer. Who is this girl? The sister he had never known. What was her name? Second sheet, two women. The younger, in low cut blouse and tight skirt, deliberately standing in profile to accentuate her figure, arching her back, holding her skirt and thrusting her left leg forward, her head turned towards the camera, one arm draped over the other's shoulder, hair lustrous, eyes alive, painted lower lip full, sensuous, her smile brilliant, brilliant in spite of – no, because of the small gap between her teeth. A woman full of life, full of sensuality, full of hope. The other, dank unkempt hair, faded diagonal patterned dress, slim frame, hollow cheeks, painful rictus grin. She clutches her sister's arm and gazes at her for strength. Haunted eyes, pinpricks, stressed into dark hollows, eyes he knows, his eyes. He looks at the photographs again. The light is brilliant; perfect. But there is something wrong. It takes him several minutes to work it out. In the first photograph a dark shadow imposes itself, draws the eye away from the image on the page. The shadow of a man, the photographer perhaps? He remembers the man, his deep foreign voice. The birthday party where he saw a green jelly rabbit for the first time and thought it was real, where they all cried after they had sung 'Happy Birthday'. His best present that day, a red Schuco car which somehow changed direction when you shouted into the grill in its roof.

And then, like crows glimpsed from a speeding train, the images have gone. He looks out of the kitchen window. Everything just as it was ten seconds ago. The line of poplars changing partners like dancers, the swaying oak, the broken swing. A thousand worlds away.

* * *

Highgate Woods. Murmurs of ancient coppiced trees, oak, hornbeam, beech. Thinning holly bushes. Gentle slopes growing imperceptibly steeper, harder, as he increases pace. Familiar, comforting exhaustion comes at last and with it an openness, an ability to see beyond the sunlight filtering through sparse branches. Beyond the filigree flashes staining the leaves and mud and paths, beyond the flicker in the eyes to the flicker in the mind.

Images invade his pounding blankness. A woman clutching his arm fiercely, scratching at him, tearing his shirt, screaming as he is dragged away. The stench of potato sacks, dust, earth in his mouth, in his nostrils. The smell of almonds and chocolate mingling with the perfume of a fairy princess; her lingering kiss; her tears, her last embrace, her wail of loss.

* * *

It is two days before he can look at the photographs again. Augustine. Augustine Rosenberg, his mother. The mother he cannot remember. Her eyes. Distraught. Destroyed, even then. And his aunt. Such confidence, such strength. The arched back, the wanton leg, the gap in her teeth. He looks again at the first photograph. The thin girl, his sister, his twin sister perhaps? The defensive arm. Did they fight? Did they share things? And this contented blond boy, was he really so happy? But where was his father? Was he that shadow in the photograph? The deep foreign voice. Why does this lawyer want to see him? To tell him how much they suffered before they died? To say they are alive? Will he see his mother, his real mother, again?

So the trap has been shut. There is no going back to the days of defensive formality, the nights of terror. He must move forward. How? Should he contact this lawyer? Tell him he is the boy in

London, 10 August 1965

these photographs? Receive reparations? Impossible. One step into the past would shatter his eggshell self, leave him as he was when he first came to England.

All those sessions trying to break free. Unhooking endless webs of pain, visualizing himself falling into nothingness, released into an emotionless void. He had drowned in amnesia for so long. Would this new knowledge destroy him? His chest is bursting. His asthma breaks through. He struggles for his inhaler.

* * *

The phone grows slippery with tears. Outside, it starts to rain – more tears trickling down the window of the sordid phone booth. Floor littered with fag ends and condoms. Stench of urine and ancient cigarette smoke, prostitutes' cards promising oblivion for an instant. He can hardly make out the endless numbers on the soggy grey Swiss letterhead. At last the receiver purrs, an unfamiliar tinny sound.

"Federiz Avocat, j'ecoute."

Young woman, indeterminate accent.

"My name is Michael Turner, Mr Federiz please, he is waiting to hear from me."

"Michael Turner – you say?

"Yes."

"I am the secretary of Mr Federiz, perhaps I can help you?"

"No I'm sorry but I must speak to Mr Federiz himself. It is very urgent."

"One moment please."

Pounding migraine. How did he get here? He had spent days deciding that he would do nothing. He was determined to wait for the agony to pass, for the images to stop invading. And then, on his way to the hospital, he found himself walking into this phone booth. Why? What possessed him?

"Mister Turner?"

A voice lacking authority. Some minor functionary, a government clerk perhaps.

"This is Doctor Michael Turner, is that Mr Federiz?"

"I am Federiz. You have receipted my letter, yes?"

"It's hardly likely that I would be ringing you otherwise, wouldn't you say?"

"I am sorry, I do not understand." A pause, "Oh, yes this is the famous English sense of humour. So Dr. Turner, are you recognizing any of the photographs I have sent you?"

"Yes, the boy, that is me. There is no doubt."

"No doubt you say. Good. Good."

"Look, Mr Federiz, I don't really want to revisit my past unless it is really necessary. I have no idea who you are and why you have…"

"…Dr Turner, of course I cannot force you to help with my enquiries. But many people have died in my country during the war, in terrible ways. I am determined to find the people who did these things, to bring them to justice. Will you help me?"

Michael cannot answer.

"Dr. Turner, are you there?"

"Yes, yes. I will. I will help you. But I cannot see how I can prove…"

"…Please Dr. Turner, say nothing more to me at this time. It is very important that you say nothing now. I will be in England within five days. I must now make an arrangement with you for the time I am in your country. We must meet. Is it OK for you?"

"I suppose so, what day?"

"Thursday fifteenth August at the Ritz Hotel in Piccadilly London, at midday? Is OK?"

"Yes, I'll ask for you at the Reception."

"Good. I will a see you in five days at the Ritz Hotel in Piccadilly London. Good bye Dr. Turner, and thank you for your gentle co-operation. Oh, one more thing. Please, do you have any photograph of yourself as a child?"

As a child? The one they took at Calais. The label round his neck. The look of terror still in his eyes.

"Yes, yes I have one photograph, from when I left France."

"Excellent. Bring it with you please. Oh, I am not sure if I said that I will also need to see your passport. Until 11am on the fifteenth then. Goodbye."

"Wait!"

Michael is stunned by the panic in his voice.

"Sorry... sorry, can you tell me please. Are any of my family alive? Is my mother alive, my sister?"

The lawyer is firm.

"I regret that I am not at liberty to divulge any information until I have personally verified your identity. I am sorry Dr Turner. This is the law. I will give you all the information on the 15th."

Michael replaces the receiver without a word. His pain is too intense.

* * *

Unusually pallid August day, polished Americans hovering around the exquisite Art Deco entrance. Why has he never noticed this beautiful glass canopy before? Why is he fixating on it now of all times? Over-dressed, embellished porters sneer behind ingratiating smiles.

Endless queue at reception. Ice forms on his forehead as he inches forward. A short man with silvering hair is looking at him, his eyes questioning.

"Mr Federiz?"

"Yes, Dr. Turner?"

Impeccable in dark suit and crisp white shirt. Florentine reds in swirling tie. Doubts intrude. It was not too late. He could give a false identity, accuse the lawyer of profiting from his grief, plead another appointment, or insanity. At least that would be nearer to the truth.

Uncomfortably deep armchair. Sipping tea from delicate porcelain. Federiz is poring over passport, driving licence, his only early photograph. The lawyer looks up occasionally, appraising, smiling constantly, reassuring, encouraging. Too smooth by half. He frowns slightly.

"What I have to tell you now, is not, how do you say it, pleasant. But you already know this. You have, no doubt, like so many others I have met, always asked yourself what happened to your parents, to your sister."

"My twin sister?"

"Twin sister. Yes….yes of course…sorry, so sorry. Tell me, do you recognise the young woman in the photograph?"

"My aunt."

London, 10 August 1965

"Yes, your aunt, Mathilde Auslander. She has been seeking you for twenty years. She resides here in London, at a special nursing home for Survivors. She was with your mother until...I have ascertained that she will talk only to Michel Rosenberg, no one else. It will be difficult for her. She knows this, but she is very ill and she wishes to...to atone for her survival."

He extends his hand.

"Here is the address and telephone number of the home. I will inform them today. They will expect your call."

Michael reaches for the piece of paper, studies it, then pauses. An unworthy thought perhaps, but he must ask.

"Forgive, my frankness Mr Federiz, but you have gone to a lot of trouble to find me, coming here to England, doing all this research. Can I...I mean, what your, your, motivation is in all this?"

The little man smiles ruefully and opens his hands.

"If your researches lead you to...to a significant material conclusion, then you will find ways of recompensing me. That is all. No contract, Just...just, as you say, a gentleman's agreement."

Federiz stands, clearly embarrassed by the turn which the conversation has taken. His hand is cold. Michael feels reassured by this change.

"Thank you Mr. Federiz. This information, it was very helpful. I have wondered, as you said, for many years about ... my escape... my, my parents. What happened to them ... to my sister. I will act on your...this address at once and write to you if I find anything out."

The lawyer's charm has evaporated.

"I must warn you Dr. Turner. You may find nothing. You may find painful things, very painful things. Be prepared for both of these eventualities."

Michael nods his head, turns and threads his way nervously through the chattering, over-dressed women filing into lunch.

* * *

The nightmare is unfamiliar. He is wrestling for his life. A dark force is pushing him, forcing him, dragging him towards a bright light. He knows he must resist. It is no use. He grows weaker and weaker. The light is searing. Blinding. He starts awake before the final moment. Tomorrow, he will see her. His aunt Mathilde. Will he be able to keep his emotions in check? Will she recognise him? 'Very ill' the lawyer said. How ill? Will it be too much for her? He must use his training to help her. To give her hope, make her live again. His sleep returns. Fitful, fractured.

CHAPTER 2
London, 16th August 1965

Discreet, bronze plaque, italicized capitals, *'CAMERON HOUSE'*. Chipped bark path winding gently through wide garden decked in summer shades. Hydrangeas with pink and blue mop heads, spiky mauve dahlias, blousy white petals hanging on precariously to tortuous, knotted rose bushes. The building itself, classic Hampstead 1890s, substantial, stately, broad, bay-windowed, Clematis mauving the deep red brick. A home, not an institution.

Ebony double door, ancient polished bell-pull. The noise sounds deep within, a hollow, jangling peel.

The door opens after an agonising five minutes. A tiny, severe-faced woman stands in the claustrophobic lobby, hand-outstretched.

"Dr. Turner? Felicity Slewitt."

She didn't need the badge, this was Matron. She had been Matron all her life.

"Thank you for being so prompt."

She looks briefly at the watch pinned to her dark blue uniform.

"Early, in fact. Good. Good. Mathilde has been preparing herself since six o'clock this morning. She is so anxious to meet you."

Michael pushes a bunch of yellow roses at her mechanically, like a five year old. She does not take them.

"Oh, you have brought her flowers, how nice. Mathilde will be pleased. But you must give them to her yourself...and you have managed to bring some sunshine with you at last. Excellent."

Her words are intended to calm him. Instead there is the urge to turn. Can he really cope with this? Is it Pandora's Box, or the way to some sort of fulfilment.

"My aunt, is she very ill?"

"She is very fragile, but her spirits have lifted considerably since she found out that you were alive and coming to see her. You will bring her joy."

The grin he has practised all the way to the Cameron House starts to crumple. The woman reaches out and takes his hand gently. She is too damn perceptive.

"Dr Turner, please forgive my presumptuousness. We have not met before, but I feel I must tell you how much I admire what you are about to do. You will help your aunt immeasurably, immeasurably. I have already detected a change in her. She has started taking an interest in her appearance, in her surroundings. You have given her hope, a glimmer of happiness, a reason to live. But at what cost to yourself? I feel instinctively that you may already have considered the risks you are taking. But are you aware of the power of the wounds you have, wounds which may have been inflicted in your early childhood? There are memories in you, memories long since forgotten, repressed. These memories may return. You are a very brave man.

Michael is embarrassed by her directness. He blurts his response.

"I am a doctor matron. If this woman were not my aunt, if she were a patient, someone I could help, I would do what I could for her. Of course I am anxious. But I am, at least I hope I am prepared."

London, 16th August 1965

She looks intently at him, her eyes fixing his.

"I am so pleased that you said that. For my part, I believe that you do have to learn the facts, that your wounds do have to be cauterised. Without that process they will seep venom forever. They may already have affected the way you relate to others. I will make you one solemn promise Mr Turner. And this is not mere wishy-washy, do-gooding stuff. It is born of experience. Once you know, really know the facts, your life will change. That shut-off part of you will begin to open. You will become more aware of who you are."

They leave the green and mauve vestibule and enter a new world, institutional, austere. The grey lino corridors smell of strong antiseptic. The lime walls hang with second-rate oil paintings. They pass through a large room open at one end to a long mature garden. High-backed chairs. Immobile, spectres, lost in their nightmares, merge into the furniture. Nurses flit to and fro, offering comfort to the most afflicted. A painting class is about to start. A brisk young man in a red sweater, bearded and skull-capped, marginally too cheery for the occasion, is handing out pallets and brushes.

A hennaed woman, apart from the rest, rehearses the agitated conversation she has repeated so often.

"We should have sold out. Why didn't we sell out and leave when we could?"

Matron breaks off to comfort her.

"Now then Sarah, you know Henrik did what he thought was best. Reuben's here to do Watercolours with you. You like Watercolours, don't you?"

The nodding face subsides to a half-smile.

The corridor is wide now, airy. Sunlight checkers the pale walls. Most doors are closed. Three are open, anxious nurses sit just outside each of them looking in, notices on the doors say 'Twenty Four Hour Watch.' They pass through a fire door. After an age, Matron stops.

"Right, here we are. Before I take you in and introduce you to Mathilde, there are a few guidelines, well, rules really. As I am sure you know, this experience will be very joyful for you both, but it will also generate painful emotions. You must at all costs be careful not to show her your pain. Remember, she has waited so many years for this moment. She has rehearsed every word she will say to you. Ask no questions. Let her speak. She will tell you only what she wants you to hear. And whatever she tells you, do not react."

She pauses, uncertain, less sure of her ground.

"There are two other matters I must raise. At this early stage it has been decided that you should not tell Mathilde that you are a doctor. We feel that this may raise her hopes unduly. Secondly, and I know that you will understand me saying this, but since you *are* a doctor, it is important that you know the treatment which your aunt is currently receiving. She is under excellent medical care. We have a team who are experienced in the various pathologies which affect her. She is also getting psychological help. She sees our resident psychiatrist every day for an hour. They have been working together for three years now. Should you wish to...to add anything to any of her treatment regimes, I am sure you will agree to discuss your ideas with our medical professionals before taking any action. Your contribution as a member of her family is

London, 16th August 1965

invaluable to her, and to us. You will make a big difference to her state of mind. But this must not be a medical contribution. Do we understand one another?"

Michael nods his head mechanically. How stupid of him to think that he would have been able to gallop in on his white steed and cure all his aunt's ills. He was only just finishing his clinical training.

Matron knocks and opens the door.

"Michel is here, Mathilde dear. He's brought you some flowers, yellow roses. Shall I show him in?"

A woman is sitting up in bed with her back to the door. There is a momentary pause. Then, a voice, high-pitched, almost coquettish.

"Yellow roses. How lovely. Yes, yes. Send him in. Send him in."

He moves round to the front of the bed and stands there holding his bouquet like an awkward lover. Matron rescues the flowers, magics a vase and hovers by the open door.

The woman has arranged herself carefully. Although the room is bathed in sunlight, she is sitting in deep shadow, a shawl carefully draped around her shoulders and across her body. The lustrous hair is still there. Blond like his, perhaps too blond. The mouth, he recognises instantly from the photograph, the full lower lip, the gap in her teeth. No longer provocative, attractive. Now the cheeks are rouged, the face thickly powdered. How old? How old can she be? Greyness lurks beneath the surface. Pain dims the pallid eyes.

He fights the need to embrace her.

She looks for a long time.

"So this is Michel. Michel alive. A man. A real man."

She seizes his hands and peers into his face for a long time.

"Yes, it is you, really you. Augustine's boy. Really you."

No hysteria, no emotion.

He tries to speak. His mind drained by the moment. He is looking at his only living relative, his aunt, his real aunt, and he has nothing to say. He sees her through layers of opaque numbness. A sound emerges from him, a strangled, animal sound.

"Yes, Michel. They are so strong, you cannot let them break through. I have lived like that for so long."

Michael's voice is hoarse.

"I am here now Aunt Mathilde. Your Michel is back. I will never leave you. Never. I will help you. I will make you happy... give you back your strength...your health."

Mathilde knows the truth. His words sound hollow, fruitless. She manages a half smile and turns to hide her pain. She motions towards a small table. Michael hands her the water glass. She sips. She has recovered herself.

"Please, please Michel, sit. Sit down. I must tell you now, It started at once. The transports were taking them each day, hundreds each day. Some of us knew. Others, your mother, she could not... too much to...."

Her voice begins to disintegrate. A whine, a half scream.

"...want to know. Of course. Must know...must. Must know..."

Matron comes in. She is firm, almost abrupt.

"I'm afraid that is enough for today. You will see Michel tomorrow, Mathilde. He will come tomorrow."

Mathilde's face collapses. She turns away in shame. He rises, hesitates, starts to say how sorry he is, remembers Matron's words, and remains silent.

London, 16th August 1965

Matron leads him out of the room and returns to give Mathilde a tablet and a glass of water.

"Michel will be here tomorrow, dear, I promise. Tomorrow. But first you must sleep. Sleep."

Matron closes the curtains, helps Mathilde to lie down and pulls the duvet over her.

He stands in the corridor. Sweat has stained his pale grey shirt a soggy black. He had forgotten to bring a handkerchief.

He leaves quickly. He needs to detach his emotions, to analyse what he has seen with his doctor's perspective. He staggers out into England's Lane. Where did he park the mini? Impersonal streets. Oblivious pedestrians. How can they not know what has happened? Why is there no hint of cataclysm in this self-satisfied world? It takes him 20 minutes to catch the flash of yellow in the sunlight. Yellow, the colour of his car, the colour of the star his aunt, his parents were forced to wear.

* * *

He has chosen his favourite circuit again. Highgate Woods. So changed from last time. No sun. Grey skies. Drizzle. Mutually sniffing dogs, middle-class mums and their muddied prams. He turns off the path, increases his pace. Familiar. Comforting. Part of his ritual. Branches snatch frantically at his head. Then comes the moment when everything stops. The heaving lungs, the elevated pulse, the dull pain in his calves, the squelch of his Green Flash shoes in the puddles. The moment when he is floating above the effort, floating in a lightness of speed. Floating and aware. Mathilde.

This woman with her mascara and her mournfulness. His aunt, his terminally ill aunt. The dark flecks in the cloudy iris. The essential tremor. The punctured breathing. All signs of extreme chemical imbalance.

'The transports were taking them each day, hundreds each day. Some of us knew. Others, your mother, she could not...'

Mathilde was there. There with him. With his mother. His sister. Her face when she caught sight of him. He has given her something. What? A chance to see that a member of her family has survived, that there will be Auslanders, Rosenbergs in the future. He must help her. He must comfort her.

* * *

This time Mathilde is more composed. She motions him silently to the chair. Again the carefully shaded face. The bed jacket arranged for maximum effect. The rouge. She takes the yellow roses and dumps them into her water jug without a second glance. Her voice is quieter, fuller.

"Michel...Ah Michel. I was so overwhelmed with joy when the lawyer said he had found you at last. So many years. So many years."

She pauses, peers at him, unsure.

He tries to break the silence, but is again struck dumb. Why can't he say something, tell her how overwhelmed he is to be in her presence? Eventually she speaks.

"I regret terribly our first encounter. I had promised myself that I would be courageous. But seeing...but seeing you, your emotions.

London, 16th August 1965

It was too much. Today we will talk about the good times, the earlier times. Please ask me, ask what you wish?"

He glances nervously at Matron, poised as before by the door. She gives no sign of disapproval. The questions crowd in.

"My parents, how..."

"Ah yes, your parents. Augustine was seven years older than me. There had been a brother, but the scarletina..."

Mathilde sips some water.

"Augustine was someone who knew only kindness, who saw only kindness in others. She even had good things to say about the *canaille* who betrayed their neighbours. She was not pretty, not a beauty like me. But she had a...a special quality. For those who recognised her sweetness, her real *bonte,* no-one was more attractive. And yet, when she felt that an injustice had been committed she could become so *feroce*. Even papa would quail before her indignation."

Mathilde's face softens. She is, at last, in a less painful past.

"I remember one day when she was 18 and I was, what, eleven maybe. She found a stray kitten in the gutter and brought it home in her *cartable,* her satchel. There was such a commotion! Papa stood firm for two whole days, but he could not withstand the onslaught, the tears, the pleas. She didn't eat a thing until he gave in. She would sit at the table, her face grey with hunger and look wistfully at him. Of course, she got her way. The kitten, Louis Napoleon we called him, stayed, stayed for a week. Then ran away.

"It was the same when she met Maurice, when she met your father. I could see at once that something had happened to her. Her eyes, they were so bright. At first she wouldn't tell me, but at last she relented. 'This one is so different,' that's all she said, 'This one is so different.' He was a lecturer, you see, at the *Ecole Normale Superieure*. Very urbane, very aloof, very ugly, very old, twenty years older than her, but so intelligent. And very religious. He even sang at a local synagogue. It was in the family, his father had been rabbi of Grodno in Lithuania. He had only been in Paris for five years. She took me to hear him once, secretly of course. Such a voice. Augustine said that there was talk of sending him to Milan to train as an opera singer, but then, when he met her..."

She breaks off and pushes herself higher in the bed, waving Michel's arm away.

"Father was *laique,* secular. He hated all that, called it, 'superstitious rubbish'. He had rejected his god, his religion, his race, in favour of a new god, Capitalism. He was a banker. The family bank, Auslander, from Vienna. Such pride, stupid pride.

"I can remember the day she brought him home. All she told papa was that she had 'met a boy' and wanted to introduce him to us all. Papa just looked at Maurice. He was speechless with rage, appalled, couldn't believe this older man had the audacity to present himself as a suitor for his beloved Augustine, refused even to shake his hand. And of course, Maurice made matters worse. He was wearing a large *kippah*, a red skullcap, such a provocation, a skullcap. Oh, he knew what he was doing, that Maurice!

"The interview lasted seconds. Mother took one look at my father and made some excuse. An urgent engagement, and they left. Augustine was beside herself. That skullcap destroyed so much... so much.

"Of course, my parents knew better than to forbid Augustine to see Maurice. It would have been impossible anyway. She was his student. They thought that it would pass. That he would grow bored with her, with this little *ingénue*. Two months later, there was a family occasion, a marriage. My cousin Hanna. Big society affair. Augustine announced, just announced to us all, that she was bringing Maurice. This time papa prevailed. He said 'No' and she couldn't move him, so she did not come to the wedding. That's when we all knew that something serious was going to happen. Or maybe it had already happened?"

The rain has stopped. The sun gilds the room. Mathilde pauses.

"Help me up, Michel. Give me my robe. I wish to go outside, to the terrace."

Michael, helps her to her feet. He is astonished at how light she is. Bird-like. Her frailty makes him anxious.

"Don't worry, Michel. I am stronger than I look. Come, sit by me, here."

This time she chooses a place in the sun. Seems, at last, almost oblivious of her appearance.

"Papa was a great 'fixer'. He got things done. Impossible things. I remember a great deal of whispering. The radio on quietly, an English station, but in French. Doors being closed, silences when we came into the room. Some sort of conspiracy. I cannot be completely sure, but I believe that my parents were thinking of sending Augustine to Switzerland, or taking us all to Switzerland because the Germans might invade at any time. She must have found out.

"One afternoon, Augustine did not come back from college. One of her classmates brought us a note. 'We have eloped,' that's all it said, 'We have eloped,' not even signed. My mother fainted of course, she could faint on demand, *maman*. Papa went pale and called an influential friend, a man who knew his way around. But by the time they were found, Augustine and Maurice were married. Married, by a rabbi. Everything had been done strictly according to Jewish law and custom. The two Jewish witnesses, the cup of wine, the breaking of the glass, the blessings, the marriage contract. No party of course, just three of their friends. Married and living in Belleville, that slum. She told papa that she was already pregnant. There was no way of knowing if she was lying, but you and your sister came along very quickly. So.....such beautiful babies. Your sister, she was never still, never happy, incessant whining, arms and legs always flailing around, such energy. And that cry. Such a cry. A cry we should have heeded. Five thousand years of suffering. But you. You were always so good. You lay there and smiled and bubbled and burbled and gurgled from the very first days."

Her eyes are gleaming. A faint light of pleasure at the sight of such innocence being brought into so corrupt a world.

"I would visit you secretly. Help Augustine to change the nappies, wash you both in their tiny sink. But she did not see papa again, not until..."

The clouds return to her eyes. Her voice flattens and grows hoarse.

"...not until she came to us. To our home. With you and your sister. Maurice was taken very early. He had written something about the Nazis in a Jewish magazine. He had no chance. No chance at all. So one afternoon, there was a telephone call. I answered it and all I could hear... crying, such weeping. The three of you, all crying. Papa and I went straight to Belleville. It was terrible. They had broken down the door, taken things, even their menorah. And it was Frenchmen who did this, Frenchmen. They had beaten Maurice in front of her. He had refused to go quietly, insisted that they show him an arrest warrant. What a fool! What an idiot! So Augustine came back to us with her cots and her babies and her nappies and her tears. It was not easy, but there were no recriminations. *Maman* was heroic. She immediately took over the care of the babies. I did my best to...I did my best with Augustine... hysterical, completely hysterical. Papa went to the *Gendarmerie* at Belleville with a friend of his, a judge, and a huge case of money. But it was no use. They could do nothing, nothing. Maurice had already been shot. We did not tell Augustine."

Matron is here. She has detected something. A change of tone? A piece of body language, perhaps? She nods to Michael firmly and he rises.

"May I come again tomorrow?"

"Yes, tomorrow. At three. There is so much you must be told. Tomorrow."

Michael looks at Matron.

Can I ask one question, just one, please."

Matron nods grudgingly.

"Just one."

"My sister, my twin sister. What was her name?"

Mathilde's face softens again.

"Rebecca. Her name was Rebecca."

"Thank you ...thank you so much."

"Yes, she was named after your great grandmother Auslander."

Michael stumbles out into a line of confident eight year-old boys wearing impeccable blazers. This is what he hates, really hates about Hampstead.

* * *

He chooses a longer, harder route this time. Hampstead Heath, steeper slopes. Ponds, paths, poodles. Kenwood House glinting and manicured in the setting sun. His mind clears as he runs, but this time there is no peace. Only realisation. Nineteen thirty nine, the year of his birth. Paris. The rumours, the terror, terror at the stories coming out of Germany. Newspapers showing shop-fronts smashed, rabbis cleaning the streets of Berlin with toothbrushes, their beards brutally torn off by brown-shirted thugs. His mother's terror even before he was born. Terror which reached deep into her womb and enveloped the two entwined foetuses. Terror which had formed him, shaped him as a child. Made him a comedian, an entertainer, a charmer. One who brought light to his parents' blackened world, one who let them see some happiness before the end. But at what cost? Could a baby really play a part, assume a role, from the earliest of times?

Augustine, his mother. A woman who saw only kindness in others. Her innate sense of right and wrong. Fierce in the face of injustice. Fragility. Stubbornness. So his was not simply learned behaviour. Genetics ruled, even in these behavioural areas. Perhaps he had inherited these characteristics? Perhaps Lamarck was not wrong after all?

* * *

London, 16th August 1965

It is as if he had never left. She is already seated under the whispering silver birch in the anaemic sunshine. Her blanket has slipped. He helps her to adjust it, before extending his bunch of yellow roses.

"Only local florists, I'm afraid."

She blushes slightly, feeding off his awkwardness.

"Yellow, such a vibrant colour. Your favourite, I think, Michel. Thank you. Thank you. Sit down, please."

This time someone has prepared a small, stone table and a vase. They are beginning to develop rituals. She grasps his wrist and guides him to a different seat. Her grip is skeletal, but unnaturally firm.

"No, not there, over here where I can see you better. Now ask your questions. Please, anything."

"You said that your father was very rich and powerful. A banker."

She smiles ruefully.

"So, if he was so rich, so powerful, why did we not escape? To the south? To America? The answer is simple. Papa was too rich, too powerful. Promises were made by...by an influential person... more than one. He never took his French nationality. We pleaded with him after the *Anschluss*, but he was adamant. Too proud of his German heritage, of what his ancestors had achieved there. Even made us learn German. We had to recite Goethe and Schiller before breakfast every morning until we were fourteen. Such blindness!"

She motions towards a glass of water. He almost spills it in his haste to help her.

"Even then papa left nothing to chance. He created a secret area. Three false rooms high in the loft. Did it all himself. Used to put the radio on very loud to hide the noise of the hammering. You could trust no-one in those days. A complete *apartement*. So well hidden. We got word from a senior policeman that we would receive a 'visit'. We all made our way to the secret area. But when they came, the Police, they knew, they knew everything. Within five minutes they were breaking down the false panel. Madame Grenier, the concierge. Too polite. Too fawning. Always sniffing around, looking at our silver, our porcelain. Picking things up. She was standing at her window as they led us out. She was the one."

She pauses. Her gaze falters. Her voice begins to crumble. He looks towards the open door. Matron is has returned, but this time she does not intervene.

"The buses were waiting, our neighbours were there, the local rabbi with his eight children. Papa could not look at him. No-one said a word. The shame had silenced us."

She shudders.

"Even now it makes me want to vomit."

"They took our parents to Drancy and we went by bus to Pithiviers with you and your sister. That bus, so ordinary, just like the one I took to work every day.

At Pithiviers it started at once. The transports were taking them each day, hundreds each day. 'A new life, work, food, food for everyone'. Some of us knew. Others, your mother, she could not... too much, too much to comprehend. She knew but she couldn't know... not that. They were taking everyone, the young, the old, the sick... everyone."

She pauses, an awkward silence. Then shakes her head as if dispelling some troublesome fly, and begins again.

London, 16th August 1965

"One day, the train was late arriving. We queued for hours. Waiting. Waiting. The train arrived. They started pushing people into those cars. Beaten and pushed. Ravaged by those huge dogs. The guards more hurried, more brutal than ever. A little girl, three, maybe four. Long brown hair, big red ribbons, green eyes, pink dress, fell from the carriage. The guard caught her by the hair before she hit the ground. She looked at him and giggled. He swung her round and hurled her with all his strength into the car, into the mass of people, into her parents. That's when I knew what...what I had to do."

Another long break, Mathilde sips some water.

"I was a beauty then. What do you say in English? 'Stunning'. Seventeen and stunning. They all wanted me. I could see it, the hunger. No-one was immune. And I loved it. I loved the power it gave me. I had a protector in Pithiviers. A powerful man, very powerful. He had connections outside. Government connections. That's why we ate. That's why we were taken so late. Only after he had been taken. Did I do wrong? My body was my only...but never the SS, never the SS. They shot all the women they went with. Forbidden you see. Forbidden to defile their bodies with... they would rape and shoot. Rape and shoot."

Her hands are fluttering. Fluttering and grasping at some unknown support.

"Rape and shoot. Rape and...I saw it...saw it...saw it so...."

Matron is there. She is calming Mathilde. Again the tablet. The glass of water. This time she only has to glance at Michael. She follows him out of the room and takes his arm as he walks.

"Dr Turner. I am sure you will forgive me, but I wish to remind you of a conversation which we had when we first met. I have had a great deal of experience in these matters, a great deal, and I have detected a change in you. When you first came you were confident. Now there is vulnerability. This story, your aunt's story is taking its toll."

Michael tries to be civil.

"Hardly surprising, wouldn't you say, Matron?"

"No, no Dr Turner, not surprising at all. But I just wanted to say that we have resources here, resources which would be available to you as Mathilde's only living relative..."

"Mathilde's only living relative that you know of."

Did he mean to be so harsh?

She pauses.

"I see your mind is made up, doctor. If you change your opinion, please let me know. This guilt that I believe you may be feeling now, it is not unusual, and there are ways of dealing with it. Well-researched techniques. Please try to remember that we are here to help."

She turns and walks quickly back to Mathilde's room.

Guilt. Survivor guilt. Is that what he is feeling? All he can feel is Mathilde's pain and a crushing sense of the randomness, the injustice of it all. No guilt. Guilt is for the Germans. He is fine. He can come through this. His training had taught him to distance himself. Now all he needs is a long run. A run into oblivion.

* * *

There is no call for three days. Then he is summoned. Mathilde is out of her bed, sitting on the terrace again. Although it is warm,

London, 16th August 1965

she is muffled in a woollen dressing gown, covered by blankets, she is quietly eating lunch. Sipping her soup. She sees him and her hand starts to shake. Does he really have such an effect on her? He takes the spoon and feeds her carefully, making sure that the soup is not too hot, that the spoon is not too full. She is meek, submissive. She slurps noisily and then smiles, for the first time since he has met her. Her face breaks with tradition. Her grin. The grin he recognises from the faded photographs, the gap in her teeth.

"So strange Michel. So strange. You are feeding me just as I fed you. Testing the temperature on the back of your hand, pouring the excess back into the bowl. Just then, I became you. I slurped my soup just like you. Now I know we are together. Really together."

She sees his reaction, reaches out and holds him to her. They embrace for a very long time.

A nurse comes in with a cup of coffee and starts pouring milk.

"Not too much milk Sabena, please."

The nurse pretends to be stern.

"Now then Mathilde darling, you tell me that every time. You know what Matron said."

Mathilde sips gently, savouring the insipid taste.

"They allow me *cafe* now, one cup a day. For years they would not let me drink it. *Cafe*, my one remaining passion. She lifts the mug to her nose and inhales deeply. *Cafe*. I would have given my body a thousand times over for a sip."

Michael shifts uncomfortably in his chair. She reacts instantly. Her speech, animated, firm.

"Sorry. I must go on.....You remember...from last time?"

Michael, nods.

"The transports would always come late in the afternoon. Only a few hundred of us were left. There was this....sacks of potatoes would arrive on a horse and cart once every few days. There was this boy...the boy who drove the cart. Philippe. He liked me. Just a boy, sixteen, seventeen maybe. Really liked me. A few minutes of pain for me, pleasure for him...a life for you.

"He would have taken your sister as well, but Augustine couldn't let her go. I tried to persuade her. I hit her, hit her hard. But it was no use. She clung so tightly. Philippe gave you Cognac, Cognac and raspberry juice. You choked at first, spat it out. Then you drank.

"Such big sacks. Such a little boy. We watched Philippe joke with the guards as they plunged their knives into the sacks again and again. He was clever. He had put you right at the top of the pile."

He can smell the rotten potatoes. The air is full of dust; of dirt. Fine powder invades his lungs, his mind. He fumbles for his inhaler. She waits, impassive.

"Your mother never forgave me for that. Those days on the train, people dying around us. Her eyes, full of venom. Such venom. Until...until the ramp. The *Selektion*. A flick of the finger and your sister was gone. Then she knew. Then she clung to me, to my strength. But she was no longer in this life. It had been too much...too much. One morning, she smiled at me, gave me her bread and died...died standing up. That was the worst, the worst."

The hands have started fluttering.

Matron's voice is firm.

"Michel must leave now. He will be back tomorrow."

Michael stands and extends his hand.

"Must you go Michel? There is so much more to tell."

Michael takes her hand and kisses it lightly.

"Tomorrow, early. I will be back tomorrow. You have my solemn word."

* * *

Mathilde's words, her very intonation, stormed his defences. 'No longer in this life' His mother, no longer in this life. Too good. Too good a soul. Destroyed by her own immutable sense of justice. Divested of life by a world of uncompromising evil.

The sacks, the smell, the sacrifice. A filthy lout entering his aunt, grunting his sperm into her body. Her defilement for his life. He spasms the horror away.

* * *

This time the garden is fragrant. It has rained overnight. A storm which shook the trellis of his balcony. She is waiting. He has forgotten the flowers.

She does not seem to notice. She sips her coffee and peers at the ancient Wisteria devouring a young Silver Birch. Strangling its branches with sinuous snakelike tentacles.

"Even plants destroy. Even plants. But you. You were not destroyed."

She knows at once. His eyes gave it away, the question.

"Of course, *mon petit,* you must be told. How could I just leave you there under the potato sacks."

Is there a glint of a smile? Is she enjoying the drama? Mathilde draws her shawl more tightly around her as the sun dims behind a solid black cloud.

"There was this woman, Madamoiselle Delphine. Delphine Garrigue. She came to live in the same apartment house as us in the seizieme. No 42, Rue Valery. So *chic,* such a *belle tournure.* Always the latest fashion, the latest *parfum*. Tall, elegant, gossamer silk stockings and those shoes, *Mon Dieu* those shoes. Lipstick, mascara...dark, dark lashes. Always a new dress, a new fur coat, a new necklace, a new *sac a main*. And the colours, Burgundy, Burnt Ochre, Crimson. I envied her so much. Made up stories about her. A Russian Princess, an American film star. And her men. So elegant, so discreet...so rich. Second floor on the left, number two, the biggest apartment of them all, with its own huge *balcon*. In the *seizieme*! Can you imagine. Our parents were scandalised, even tried to persuade our neighbours to get her removed.

"You had only met her once, Michel. After you had come back to stay with us. Your mother was desperately trying to get a visa for America or Australia, standing in a queue for hours with Rebecca. You were bored, so I took you to Madame Gautier's shop. The patisserie on the corner. That was the only time, but it was enough. You were angelic, a cherub with your golden tresses. As long as your sister's, as long as Rebecca's. You were skipping around the shop, squealing with delight and then you saw her and you stopped. You were bewitched."

He remembers the moment. A fairy queen, glittering with diamonds and rubies, seen through the mists of cinnamon and caramel...a sensual wonder of smells and tastes. He had always thought of it as a dream, an escape from the nightmares, but now...

London, 16th August 1965

"She lifted you high into the air and kissed you full on the mouth. A long kiss. I was so shocked!"

The perfume came first, roses and violets. Then the softness of her fur as it brushed his face. Then the kiss itself, her lips on his. Painfully exquisite. Could he really remember the tingle, the softening of his loins, even at that age?

"She told you she would buy you one cake. That you must choose one cake, just one. You were so careful, careful even then. She was delighted by the way you frowned and considered each item in turn. Looking at it, smelling it. You were unable to choose between *Galettes, Jocelynnais* and *Pains aux Chocolat*. You had never tasted any of them before. Finally you fixed on *Jocelynnais*."

Jocelynnais. The tiny, tantalising slivers of dark chocolate, the almonds, the light buttery crispness.

"She was your only hope, our only hope. I had no choice. I whispered her name and address to Philippe as I kissed him goodbye. I promised him more pleasures if he delivered you safely and brought me a sign. I never got that sign. I never saw him again. The transports took us the next day. All those years. All that time I never knew whether you had survived, whether the concierge had betrayed you as she betrayed us. Until the lawyer's letter. All those years thinking you were dead."

Sabena comes in with some more coffee for Mathilde.

"Is there anything I can get for you Dr. Turner, a cup of tea perhaps?"

Mathilde's eyes widen.

"A doctor? You are a doctor? Why did you never tell me?"

"Well, I have passed my second MB and nearly finished my clinical training, but there's still a long way to go."

"Augustine always used to say she wanted you to be a doctor. We made fun of her, such a conventional Jewish thing to want. So *bourgeois*. She would have been overjoyed, overjoyed. A doctor. My Michel. But there is something you must see."

Shamelessly she throws off her blanket and thrusts her left leg out from her dressing gown in a distorted travesty of that original photograph, the lawyer's photograph. The wanton leg. He remembers that shapely leg pushed out from her skirt. He remembers her smile, her vibrancy, her hope. Now the leg is disfigured, the calf scarred beyond recognition by two long scars, still livid, a parody of smiling lips.

Michael leans forward and instinctively feels each of the ridges with his fingers, testing their texture, their depth.

"Who did this to you, Mathilde?"

"The SS doctors, two of them, came to me every day for a week. Injections. For some research project."

"And how did you feel just afterwards? Do you remember."

"I remember the pain, I remember that I could hardly walk. I remember they were seeping. My friends used to carry me to *appel* and hold me up when we had to stand in the snow."

"Did they talk about your arm at all, doing the injections into your arm?"

Mathilde frowns.

"Yes, yes. I remember now. There was an argument. One of them wanted to do them in my arm. The other made him do it here. But I do remember them taking blood from my arm every day for weeks afterwards. Lots of blood."

"Did you feel ill in any other way?"

"No, not ill, not ill like that. Those feelings came later, much later, after we had been liberated. A year after we had been liberated. That's when I started to feel really ill. At first they said it was emotional, just the trauma of the camps. Years later they said that they did not know why I felt so bad, that they needed to know what had been used in the injections."

Michael is intense, almost harsh.

"And have they been able to find out what these injections were? Did they mention the word hepatitis at all?"

"No-one would tell my doctors anything. The pharmaceutical companies who paid for the experiments wouldn't tell us what chemicals had been used, wouldn't even admit they had done wrong. Why? Why? The war was over. The Jews had survived. Why did I...do I, have to endure such suffering?"

Rage boils behind Michael's eyes. Doctors. Men trained to heal, to alleviate suffering, 'Above all do no wrong'. Toxins. Mathilde's body defiled again, entered again, polluted again. First the potato lout and now these traitors to his profession, condemning her to perpetual suffering, a half-life, a life of hopelessness. And these companies, these pharmaceutical companies with their rigorous science, their pompous hypocrisy and their ingratiating representatives. Had he used drugs made by the company which refused to help Mathilde? What can he do now, after so many years?

"These men, Mathilde, do you remember anything about them?"

"Only that one was very good-looking."

She pauses for a moment.

"But, you Michel. Now you are here, perhaps you can help me. Find what poison they used. At least do something about the pain, the weakness. Please."

Michael remembers Matron's words,'She is under excellent medical care. We have a team of doctors who are experienced in the various pathologies which affect her.'

He holds Mathilde's hands in his. His voice is low, shamed.

"Oh Mathilde, I only wish I could help you. But I have not even fully qualified yet. These people who are treating you, they are experts. They have worked with others like you. I can do very little. I will talk to them, I promise. But...but I cannot help. I cannot really help."

Mathilde turns away from him. She is crying. Her grip on his arm has tightened. She has been searching his face for reassurance. And then with realisation, comes despair. Her hands are fluttering again.

Matron is here. She wheels Mathilde back into her room.

"That's quite enough for today dear. You need to rest."

Michael finds his voice at last.

"Goodbye *tante* Mathilde."

She looks at him sharply.

"Do not call me that, ever. *Tante* Mathilde! *Tante* Mathilde makes me sound old. I am not old, not old at all. I am 36, that is not old! You are old. Old before your time, with your dark suit, your schoolboy hair, your thick glasses, your blushes. You are worse than old."

Her face is suffused with blood, with rage.

London, 16th August 1965

"And I do not want to see Michel. Michel *le medecin,* again. It is enough. I cannot endure the pain. Michel must not come back. Not come back!"

Matron, is unhurried. Her voice calm, soothing.

"Mathilde my dear, I am sure you do not mean that. We will discuss things tomorrow, when you are feeling better."

Matron nods firmly at Michael. He backs out slowly.

"Goodbye Mathilde. I am sorry. So sorry."

"*Adieu* Michel."

She says the words bleakly without looking up.

* * *

That evening his running punishes. He tortures his body. He flails the paths with his feet. And as he runs, his mind lashes him. Such stupidity, such pathetic stupidity! He knew she was volatile, he knew she was vain. Did all his years of training mean nothing? One word, one simple word, had cost him the only chance he would ever have of helping her. The woman who had given her beautiful young body to save his life. How could he have been so crass? How? What can he do? Can he atone for his mistake? Yes. Find Delphine. Take Delphine to see her. She will forgive you if you manage to do that.

CHAPTER 3
Paris, 2nd September 1965

The sign reads *Gautier et Cie, Chocolaterie et Patisserie*. A new sign, gold capitals on nasty plastic electric blue. A corner shop. In one window, pyramids of chocolates, luminous blue packages adorned by gold bows, small golden packets, blue ribboned and carded, instant recourse for the anxious lover, the apologetic husband, the forgotten birthday. The other window laden with salivating mini tarts, *citron, tatin, abricot*. Two small circular tables, blue and gold of course, on the narrow pavement, vying with prams and pedestrians. Michael enters and instantly feels the loss of something... of what? Of his childhood perhaps.

A teenage girl, outfitted in the same vicious blue and gold trim, lounges behind the counter. Michael orders some *jocelynnais* and a *chocolat chaud*. The girl is efficient, polite, but mirthless. The tastes are disappointing, too sweet somehow. The magic has gone. He can see that the *Chocolaterie* section is quite new. From this angle the pyramids look even more enticing. Their names speak of France's former glory, *Royale, Noblesse, Antoinette, Louis D'Or*, or appeal more directly to the gourmet *Amandine, Paganini Hazelnut, Cerise, Pistache, Praline*. But the counter has been changed to accommodate this excess. The shop is no longer as he remembered it. It has become asymmetrical, unbalanced.

He had hoped that the smells would remind him, bring something back, but he feels nothing – only the same great emptiness. He sits out on the street collecting his thoughts, deciding what to say. The traffic noise is too loud, the fumes too intrusive. He finishes his drink and goes to pay. A youngish man is at the till, wearing that insidious blue and gold. The man is his age, with a shock of red hair, but much taller and more at ease with himself. Michael pays the bill fumbling with the money and his bad French. The shopkeeper is condescending, but his accent is appalling.

"It is alright monsieur, you can speak to me in English."

He points to a sign indicating that English, German, Italian and Spanish were spoken.

Michael smiles.

"I see you are a bit of a linguist."

"I am sorry monsieur, this word linguist, I do not understand."

"It's just...I am impressed that you speak so many languages."

"These days, we have to be knowledgeable monsieur. So many tourists."

"Of course."

Why had he not planned what he was going to say? He was getting embarrassed, awkward.

"Yes, monsieur? Do you wish to purchase something else. Chocolates perhaps? We have the best chocolates in all Paris. Made here in our workshop, like the cakes."

Michael stammers.

No, no, it's not that. It's just....I used to come here when I was a small child with my...my...my mother, Madame Garrigue."

Paris, 2nd September 1965

The colour rises instantly in the young man's cheeks.

"Madamoiselle Delphine! Wait. Wait one minute. I will call *maman*."

The response from the back of the shop is immediate. A shriek, a torrent of French. A small round woman, Disney grandma, roly-poly with half-rimmed glasses and grey bun pinned by blue and gold clasp, bustles into the shop and lunges herself at Michael, powdering his dark suit with her whitened hands and apron. She kisses him on both cheeks, then holds him at arms length, then kisses him again, gabbling non stop.

"Michel, le petit ange, sa mascotte, Michel, Mon Dieu, quelle histoire!"

"The monsieur does not speak French *maman*. English, only English."

Maman is puzzled.

"But how is that possible, Eric? Michel spoke perfect French. Perfect."

She turns.

"You were here every day with Madamoiselle Delphine. Every day. Always the same. *Jocelynnais.*"

Michael tries to recover his composure.

"I was…I was taken away to England. To London, just after the war. When I was seven."

The woman's face pales and darkens. She removes her glasses and wipes them furiously.

"Of course. Of course. You were the Jew. The Jewish boy she saved. The one they took away from her. After all she had done – after she had risked her life. So cruel. So cruel. She was, how you say, *desolee*."

He has a wrenching memory of a woman clutching him and screaming, of two men dragging him away. Adamant, unmoved.

"And do you know where she is now, Madame Gautier? Is she still in Paris?"

The face lightens again, the glasses and twinkle are back.

"But of course. She comes to visit every month for her *petit fours*. She always tells me 'No-one can make *petit fours* like Amelie Gautier, no-one'."

There is a pause, she is dredging up a memory.

"Yes, yes, I remember. She is living at the Hotel de Buci, Rue de Buci, in the *sixieme*.

Tears start into his eyes. *Maman*. He will see her again.

"Thank you madame. Thank you so much. I will go now, take the Metro to..."

"...*Odeon*. That is the nearest. You will find it ..."

Eric breaks in.

"*Non non*, the best Metro is *St.Germain*. You will have no roads to cross. The Rue de Buci is very short. And there is a market, wonderful food, *Le Marche de Buci*."

He notices Michael's map of Paris.

"Ah, I see you have your *Indispensable*. Good, very good. Oh and this is for you."

He extends two large bags full of chocolates and cakes.

"No, no you are too generous."

Eric pulls him to one side and speaks quietly turning away from his mother so that she cannot see his lips.

"Please. It is for me....you see I was not very nice when we were little... so jealous. We used to play together and I...Once I took some of your toys."

"Tu crois que je suis trop veille pour entendre ce que tu dis!"

Madame Gautier is suddenly taller than her son.

"I am not deaf you know! *Va a ta chambre, tout de suite!*"

Eric's shoulders sag. He slinks off, crimsoned, humiliated. Madame Gautier grasps Michael's arm.

"Wait. Wait one moment. Please. There is something you must have. A letter you must have."

She returns in a second holding a small buff envelope. The Swastika is faded but clearly visible. He opens the envelope. Yellowing paper, Dutch Red Cross. No 157382 Sender Auslander Mathilde, 42, Rue Valery, Paris 16e.

"Your aunt sent me this...from the camps...one of the camps.

He reads the message. *'Tout va bien ici. J'espere que le petit gateau se vendent plus que jamais. Ecrivez svp. Mathilde Auslander.'*

Madame Gautier takes the paper from him.

"'All is well here. I hope that the little cake is selling more than ever. Write please. Mathilde' "

She gives him back the letter.

"Keep it. Keep it please."

Michael has to ask.

"And did you... did you reply?"

Madame Gautier is flustered.

"The Police came you see...and the Gestapo. They questioned me for hours, wanted to know why she referred to *'le gateau'* singular not *'les gateaux'*, the cakes. They thought it was code. I said it was just a grammatical error. I told them nothing. Nothing, even though I knew. But, no, I did not reply to the letter. That would have put my family in grave danger, you understand. Grave danger. I did not reply."

CHAPTER 4
Paris, 3rd September 1965

The lunch-time crowd spews him from the Metro St. Germain into a disorientating melee of traffic and diesel fumes. The huge edifice of a church looms, ancient, ominous, dark, casting a claustrophobic shadow over the posters and beggars lining the railings. He is lost. Well, there's only one thing for it, he will have to ask. He sees a very pretty girl in a tiny mini skirt staring at him, waving her handbag. At least she's likely to be helpful. His French is returning now. *"Pour allez a la Rue de Buci, s'il vous plait, Madamoiselle?"*

She seems startled by his question. Is he serious, or is this English humour?

"Cross here and then walk that way for twenty metres. You will see Le Marche de Buci on your left...."

She pauses.

"...and is there anything else I can help you with monsieur? Anything at all?"

He realises his mistake, reddens and hurries away to hide his embarrassment, darting into the stream of hooting traffic, mumbling incoherent apologies.

* * *

Le Marche de Buci takes him completely by surprise. It is as if he has stumbled into a different dimension of time and place. Every inch of the road and pavement is crammed with food. Bulging bunches of white asparagus and huge marrows vie for position with vast carrots and sprouts. Live lobsters in their tanks are snatched by clever hands for harried housewives. He wonders at the array of *Charcuterie,* hanging loins, rillettes and sausages, at the immaculate fish, so aesthetically arranged. Whitebait, sardines, plaice, red mullet, sole, salmon, sea bass, skate, halibut. Row after row according to size and colour. At huge jars of olives, *'Goutez monsieur. Allez, c'est gratuit'.* At the mounds of walnuts, almonds, cashews and pistachios. At the array of cheeses. Were there really six different types of Blue Cheese in France? At the steaks and livers and racks of lamb and paper thin veal fillets and sheep's heads and cow's brains. At the tiny wood strawberries, brilliant apples, succulent pears. At the superb display of fossils and shells in a corner shop. And where there is a micron of space between the stalls, a farmer's wife sits with her basket of plums or raspberries. Behind the stalls, the *traiteurs'* shops have laid out the whole gamut of enticing food, vats of *Provencale* chicken, egg tartlets with *Sauce Hollandaise,* Souffles, Quiches, Noisettes of Lamb in a Garlic Cream Sauce, *Pommes Lyonnaise.* An old man with hundred year old face is selling beautifully crafted wooden handled knives. The smells assail the palette. A whiff of *fois gras* here, a hint of fennel there, a gust of over-ripe *Brie.* A cohort of invitations to satisfy the senses. And the sounds. The sounds of a thousand markets through the centuries. The traders exhort, cajole, encourage. The shoppers, lines of expert women complete

Paris, 3rd September 1965

with red, green and blue plastic port-cullis holdalls, argue back, bargain, gossip, pay.

He navigates the narrow space behind the back of the stalls. The neon sign is illuminated. 'Hotel de Buci' within a strange medieval shield. Two stars. The entrance is tidy, functional. Stone floor, marbled black and white. Wine art deco sofas. Repro Louis Quinze desks and chairs. A small circular table, dingy and ringed, spoils the illusion. In the corner an alcove and reception counter. Smoke curls into the air from an abandoned Gauloise. He rings the bell, one timid ring. A trim, observant young woman in jeans arrives instantly.

"Madame Garrigue, *s'il vout plait.*"

"Ah yes, she is expecting you. Take a seat please monsieur, I will tell her you are here."

He sits. Then jerks upright. He has brought her nothing, nothing after all these years, after all she did.

"Wait!"

The young woman looks up, astonished at his abruptness. Her hand is poised ready to dial.

"Sorry. Sorry. I need to get something...some flowers for Madame. Please do not ring her until I am back."

"Certainly monsieur."

The woman smiles sympathetically,

"Five minutes, turn left out of the hotel, four shops down on this side of the road. They have fresh and dried flowers there."

The florists is full. He waits. Panic growing. His turn comes sooner than he expected. He has made no decisions.

"Can you choose for me? A large bouquet."

There follows a long and convoluted argument as to what flowers they should use.

"This is a lady you know well, monsieur?"

"No...well yes, once. Maybe you know her, Madame Garrigue?"

Oh Madamoiselle Delphine! Yes of course. We know just what she likes."

The process of selecting, preparing and wrapping the flowers takes an age, but the bouquet is tremendous, effulgent. He stumbles back to the hotel, laden with the bulk of the florist's produce. Delphine is already there talking to the receptionist. A trickle of memory returns. Fierce red hair, now stylishly short. Tiny, doll-like features. Long neck. Small, yet somehow statuesque, almost forbidding, a compactness, a self-contained quality, still aware of her charm, her power to attract... and outwardly calm.

She gives a slight start when she first sees him, but hides it instantly.

"So Michel, at last you have found me."

She extends her hand and takes the flowers. No histrionics, no Gallic displays, no fulsome kisses. She is hiding a great hurt, a great pain.

He hesitates, what should he call her?

"Yes Michel, it is difficult, but Delphine, call me Delphine. That will be perfectly acceptable."

Her English is formal. Accented, but confident.

"You have become a man Michel, but not a very happy one I fear."

He blushes. To his surprise he finds that his palms are prickling, almost moist. A fleeting image of crumpled playing cards invades.

Delphine moves towards him, embracing him carefully but warmly. The perfume, the same perfume. To his disgust he is aware of her breasts, still firm, still full. A single lost tear trickles slowly down his left cheek. She leads him gently to a chair.

"Will you take some coffee?"

He never drinks coffee, but simply nods his head, searching his pockets. Again he has forgotten his handkerchief. She produces a tissue and he blows noisily.

"Now that's a sound I do remember."

She smiles.

"I always used to wonder how so loud a noise emanated from so small a nose."

She gives him a wad of tissues.

"For later."

"Thank you *maman*......Delphine."

She turns to face him squarely,

"So first, I must apologise for my...for my rudeness. I should have been more...welcoming. But seeing you like this, a grown man, a serious young man, after, after so many years, brought back the day that they took you. Snatched you from me. Wouldn't even let you take your teddy bear. Brutes. I understood of course, so much anger at that time, so much pain. But after what I..."

Delphine's voice tails off. She had promised herself she would not talk about the risks she had taken. But it is too late.

"After what you had done Delphine. After you had risked your life. You could have been shot."

She looks away.

"Please Michel, I don't wish to discuss this...this matter. It is past. It is so much in the past."

"I understand, er Delphine, but tell me one thing and we will never discuss it again, just one thing."

"I know what you want to ask me. Why? Why did I do it? Why did I risk so much? I had met you only once. *Enfin*, it is easy to explain. I was a *petit bourgeois*. For les *petits bourgeois* there was no choice, no option."

"Many *petits bourgeois,* did not behave like you."

She shrugs.

"Are you sure there was nothing else?"

"Nothing."

A distant memory catches her by surprise.

"I have just remembered something. Another reason perhaps. Strange that it never occurred to me before today. Very strange. You see, my great grandparents come from Albi, in the south west of France. There was a great *massacre* there about seven hundred years ago. I think they killed 200,000 people. My ancestors, my people, the Cathars. Of course some escaped, some converted to save their lives. But many died, for their religion, for their identity. This was told to me when I was, what...sixteen maybe. My father made it very, graphic, the babies and pregnant women, all murdered. He made me promise never to forget it. Always to be aware of my heritage. Perhaps I felt that my fate was bound up with yours. But for an accident of time and place, I would have been...? Perhaps ? I do not know."

"...And the incident in the patisserie?"

She is distracted.

Paris, 3rd September 1965

"Well yes, perhaps that had affected me. You were such a beautiful child. Even before that day you had already captivated me. I saw you skipping into the hall, your smile, it was infectious. And then the patisserie, the *jocelynnais*. The serious way you went about choosing that one cake, *adorable*. I had dreamt about you every night since we met. The son I never had. And *tout d'un coup*, there you were at the back door, crying, holding the hand of that boy, covered in dirt and smelling of potatoes."

"Did that boy, the potato boy, tell you why he had brought me to you?"

"He was in too much of a hurry. He just said something like, 'This is for you,' and ran."

"He didn't tell you who had persuaded him."

"No, I just assumed it was your mother."

"It wasn't my mother, she didn't want me to go. She couldn't see what was happening. My aunt Mathilde, the woman who took me to the patisserie, she remembered you. She remembered what happened. She knew that it was my last chance, my only chance."

"That beautiful creature. I remember being so jealous of her animal power."

"She survived. That's how I found you Delphine. She is very ill. She never recovered from..."

Delphine starts with a new pain, a new realisation of horrors she had long ago put aside. Michael cannot stop himself. He presses on.

"Did you have any idea how this youth had been...been persuaded to take me from the camp?"

"I just assumed that someone had bribed him."

"They had no money. It had all been taken by the police."

The implication is not lost on Delphine. She starts to cry softly, dabbing her eyes with a tissue. It takes her several minutes to recover. Then she takes out her compact, dabs her face with powder and applies some lipstick.

"This must have been so devastating for you to hear, Michel. Terrible... terrible. I must meet her, your aunt, tell her how much I admire her."

She gives a little shake as if to free herself of these demons, and attempts a smile.

"Let us talk about you now. Michel, Michel *ma petite mascotte*. Tell. Tell me all."

Michael is dumb again – shy, tongue-tied. He reddens.

"OK, I will be more specific. What are your hobbies?"

"I love to run..long distances. The endorphins you know, so calming."

"And solitary. That is good, good for you. Endorphins... so you have some connection with medicine."

"I am a doctor. Well, I have passed my second MB and I am in my third clinical year. I hope to qualify very soon."

"Your family would have been so proud. A doctor, such an honourable profession."

Is she mocking him? A Jewish doctor, a cliché. No, she is serious.

"And have you decided your... how do you say, special area?"

She sounds like the Jewish women he has to treat, as soon as they hear he is a doctor and Jewish, they start to pry. If they don't have a daughter themselves, they're bound to have a friend who does. Perhaps there are no cultural differences after all. He looks into the distance.

Paris, 3rd September 1965

"Oh sorry Michel, if I am being too intrusive, I apologise."

"No really, it's OK, really. Actually I'm not sure yet, psychiatry probably, I have been doing a lot of reading, the usual I suppose, Freud, Jung, Adler, Charcot."

Delphine is intrigued.

"Charcot, the Frenchman, the hypnotist. Can you do it? Have you tried? Have you tried putting other people in your power? Controlling them?"

This is an accusation he has heard many times. Hypnotism as an emotional crutch, a way of putting himself beyond his insecurities.

"One or two of us have had a go. On each other. Strictly unprofessional of course."

"So how does it work? It looks so ...such dark forces."

He bristles again, the colour rising into his forehead.

"A sort of necromancy? Actually, I hadn't thought of that. I don't quite see myself as a Svengali character. I always felt the film was a rather naive piece of anti-Semitic propaganda."

Delphine is astonished at his reaction. This young man, so intense, so ready, no, so keen to be hurt, so changed from her trusting Michel, her *petite mascotte*.

"I agree, it comes from a place of hatred of bigotry, the same hatred as *l'affaire Dreyfus.*"

He knows he has over-reacted, this makes him even more embarrassed. His palms prickle again. Delphine sees the reaction and takes his hand.

"Michel, *mon cher,* I have been insensitive. Please forgive me."

He is seized with the need to take his hand away. He snatches it back too quickly. He is unused to such warmth, such openness.

"It's just...I'm a bit out of my depth, you know. This is all very..."

"For me too. But I would really like to know how it works, this hypnotism, scientifically, I mean."

Michael is on safer ground now.

"It's all to do with a small physical shock. You need to unbalance your subject and get under his guard before he recovers. A slightly aggressive handshake, pulling the subject towards you unexpectedly, just before you fix them with the hypnotic gaze. Anything like that works well."

I hope you haven't tried it on any of your girl-friends Michel?"

Michael is horrified.

"Of course not. That would be completely immoral."

"But there are some girls?"

"Well yes, a few."

Delphine seems impressed,

"A few?"

Michael is awkward. He cannot tell her the truth.

"Just one really, a special one, but it is over now."

Delphine sighs.

"The dubious pleasures of young love."

She rises.

"We will go to lunch now. I will re-introduce you to the delights of *la cuisine francaise.*"

* * *

Delphine is clearly a valued customer. She is greeted by the *patron* with great flourish. Incongruous formalities for so tiny a bistro crammed between two large fabric shops and already brimming with noisy clients.

She does not introduce Michael. Is she ashamed of him, this nervous Englishman? Her table stands ready, an alcove at the very back of the corridor-like space. She orders for them both without asking. A throw-back perhaps to those early days. Should he mind?

"Pour nous deux, Terrine maison, Contrefillet a point, haricots vert... et une bouteille de rouge, vin de maison, comme d'habitude, s'il vous plait."

He hesitates. OK, so he wasn't a vegetarian, or kosher. He decides to go along with it. But he could do with a plate of chips. Delphine is too good at reading him.

"Oh sorry, you would like some *frites*, I'm sure."

"No, no it's alright really, watching my weight."

She places her elbows on the table and cradles her face. Her eyes are searching.

"So now I want to hear everything, *Monsieur le presque Docteur.*"

Is she teasing? He can't tell.

"What is your very first memory? What do you remember of our time together?

"There's not much to tell really, Delphine. Just a few snatches. The odd image. The patisserie, I remember that. Oh, and you joking with the German soldiers in the guard-post on the corner when you walked me to school. But the rest...very little."

Her face darkens.

"And our parting? Your journey to England?"

Dim images invade. A girl with a label round her neck, both of them crying, stamping their feet to keep warm. The train. His terror when he saw it. But this time there was no shouting, there were no dogs. The boat journey where he was so sick and the girl kept wetting herself. The cliffs, the clouds.

"I think I was nearly sea-sick on the boat. But it was OK, you know. Then meeting my ...my new parents. Father with his jokes and bow tie and black suit. "

He remembers them. Two people, one tiny, the other tall, erect. He remembers the woman's fur coat, the make-up, the impossible high heels, the awkward attempt at a one-armed hug. Mother at her warmest. Father, coatless in the cold, Beaming at him, huge and immaculate in strange round hat, one he had only ever seen in Charley Chaplin films.. His nose shiny, his eyes glowing with emotion, with affection. He remembers being swept off his feet into the arms of this man, the bear hug. Real warmth. He remembers the pain in their eyes. Pain for him. Instant devotion to a creature who did not exist. Why did they pity him? He did not want their pity. He wanted *maman*. He wanted to go home. He remembers the big black car, smooth in the driving rain. He remembers the house, the absence of toys, of colour. He remembers the despair.

Delphine reaches into her handbag and produces a single letter tied with a blue ribbon. She hands it to Michael. He opens it and reads. It is a child's handwriting, several crossings-out, ink smudges, tears perhaps. The French is quite easy.

'Mummy, I want to come home. Why have you left me with these people? Mrs Faigenblum is so cruel to me. She makes me eat steamed fish and shouts at me when I can't. She's got this huge spoon. She pushes the food into my mouth and holds my nose until I swallow or choke. Father threw a whole plate of my fish in the fire the other day. He is kind. Please take me home. I want to go home. Come for me today...please, please.'

There is a note scribbled in English at the foot of the same letter.

'Thank you for all you have done for Michael, madame. Please do not respond to his letters. It will be too upsetting for the little boy if he is constantly reminded of his life in France. He is English now. It is best that he forgets the past.' The signature is indecipherable.

The food rises in Michael's throat.

"So that's why you never replied to any of my letters."

"I received only one Michel. They must have destroyed the rest. To spare me the pain perhaps."

"One letter, *maman*, just one letter of goodbye. I would have understood. I was seven!"

"But what could I have done? I think they would never have given you any of my letters. Maybe it was for the best. If you were so angry at me, you would forget me sooner."

"I never forgot you. Never."

Delphine produces a tissue from her handbag and blows her nose silently.

"It broke my heart *mon cher*, broke my heart. I would lie in bed crying. My tears would fall on your photograph. Broke my heart a second time."

She recovers herself quickly.

"Let us not talk of such matters. Later. Later when you had got accustomed to your new life. How was it later?"

Images return. The entertaining. The house full of people. Endless parties. Mother shouting when he stole a smoked salmon bagel from the bottom of the huge, carefully constructed pyramid. Dad always so jolly, always fun, always telling jokes, stories. Michael, the star attraction. Dressed up and stuffed like a turkey.

The sighs of the overweight women. His stinging cheeks. The pain of so many pinches. The agony of so many kisses. Kalookie. The night he was allowed to join in. Soggy hands. Ruined cards. Mother's screams. Dad jumping up and knocking over his chair. Leading him gently to his bedroom. Sitting with him. Cuddling him. The sound of people leaving quietly. Her words wafting up the stairs.

'Just a bit shy. Been through a lot. But he'll be alright. Sorry to break it up so early.'

The symptoms return. His hands begin to prickle again, in seconds they are pouring with sweat. The sweat of an eight year old. He wipes his palms mechanically with one of Delphine's tissues.

"Dad was my only fixed point. He loved me. Really loved me. Mother? I think maybe they took me in as a way of saving their marriage. She didn't bargain for a competitor. Later, when I was growing up it was hard for them."

"In what way?"

"They were not prepared for an angst-ridden teenager. That... that's where things really broke down between us."

The incomprehension on their faces when he raged at them. They had given him everything. He gave them hatred.

"I was pretty disgusting at that time. Arrogant and dismissive of their way of life."

She sips her wine. Her eyes are twinkling.

"And now. My little *psychiatre*. What are your feelings now? What emotions come to the surface when you, what is the technical term, ah yes, when you project back to those times with your new parents?"

Paris, 3rd September 1965

His hands moisten again.

"To be honest Delphine, I can't get in touch with any of those feelings. I am completely cut off from them. Of course my training tells me that they would have been very powerful, probably too powerful. But they have gone. Totally erased, or repressed. No doubt that is why I am getting so tense."

He wipes his hands as if to sear the skin. She relents. She has gone too far. She must be more careful.

"Cher Michel, of course it must have been traumatic for you. So let's talk about another aspect of your life. You were back in the arms of a Jewish family. Back with your religious heritage. Did you learn to love your religion?"

Religion. The word conjures a half-life. Obsessive adults with their own particular household god, the rabbi. The rabbi with the thin red hair and that vein on his temple. That vein which throbbed whenever Michael made a mistake. Strange new symbols and guttural sounds. The all-pervading presence of their God. Unforgiving. Vengeful. The cane on the back of his legs when he was naughty in *cheder*. The endless prayers. The coldness of the synagogue in winter. Each man swaying, wrapped in his shawl, wrapped in his prayers, wrapped in himself. The strictures, so obscure, so inconsistent. The dead day – Sabbath. No electricity or carrying or cooking or music or running or playing or comics. Just prayers and study, prayers and study.

But that's not fair. There was another side. He forces himself to think of the good times. So few positive memories. Then they come. Fleeting images of uncle Max. Uncle Max with his beard and his beatific grin. Uncle Max who was always humming a prayer under his breath. A prayer which brought light to his eyes, to his soul. The house. A chaos of noisy children, untidy, unkempt, bristling with joy and crumbs. The smells of stale cabbage and chicken soup. Passover at Max's house. The arguments about the wicked son, the laughter, the wine, the songs deep into the night. Going home at midnight warm and muddled.

Yes, it was uncle Max who taught him his Barmitzvah. Infinitely patient no matter how many times he got it wrong. His Barmitzvah. The horror of the day itself. His parents, more nervous than him. The synagogue, full of people he did not know. The singing of his portion, his voice switching from soprano to hoarse bass as he tried to remember the intricate melodies. The speech to his friends and family. His mother berating him in front of all the guests for stammering so badly.

Delphine is looking at him strangely.

"Oh sorry, sorry. I was distracted for a moment. Religion? Well, you know, I'm a scientist. It doesn't really impinge much now. I mean, well I... I just don't think about it a lot any more."

Her voice chokes.

"You have lost your religion? Your Jewishness?"

"My Jewishness? No, I have not lost that. I cannot lose that. My Jewish identity will always be a part of me, always."

She is standing, trembling, whispering harshly.

"And your God?"

"My God."

"Yes, your God. You do believe in God, the God of your forefathers?"

He stands.

"Look, I'm sorry, this isn't going the way I...maybe if I come back tomorrow, we can start again."

She is aware of her posture, her anger. She subsides into her chair.

"No, no. It is my fault. I became too emotional. It is...we French just get too carried away sometimes. It is in our nature. That is why politics and religion are forbidden subjects at the dinner table."

She attempts a wan smile.

"Bad for the digestion, you know. But please, tell me. What is the view you, you the scientist, the Jewish scientist, have of God?"

He thinks carefully. He does not want to alienate this woman, his saviour. Should he lie? No, she is too intuitive, she will spot that at once.

"OK. If you are asking me, do I believe that there is a sort of 'Supreme Being' who annihilated millions of his own, his 'chosen' people in the most obscene, the most pernicious, the most evil, yes, evil way, then the answer is no. But do I believe in a Spiritual force beyond our understanding? Then the answer is yes."

Delphine is calmer. This is territory she enjoys, intellectual argument, discourse.

"So there is no specifically Jewish God."

"Alright then, the Socratic method. Let us suppose, just suppose for the purposes of this argument that there is a Jewish God who led 'His' people out of the land of Egypt and spread them along the shores of the Mediterranean, throughout Europe, and beyond. A God who locked this same group of 'His' people into intellectual hothouses and made them interpret and argue over the same texts for hundreds of years, who then released them into the modern world where they used this facility with words and reasoning, to take positions of power, influence and prestige, who made them the first mercantile nation, the first true capitalists?"

Delphine smiles. Her Michel has a brain, she always knew he was clever.

"Let us also assume that, on a whim say, he decided to...how shall I put this...to gather his people to him, to his heavenly kingdom, so he could be closer to them. Why then... tell me this... why then would he arrange for so many of them to be murdered in the most obscene way possible... the most..."

Delphine interrupts.

"Surely all murder is obscene. Murder is murder."

"No Delphine, murder is not just murder! He, the mighty one, could have given them some disease, say an influenza outbreak like the 1918 pandemic. Or an ethnic disease like Tay Sachs. Instead 'He' chose...if it was him...which incidentally I do not, positively do not, believe. He chose that they should die in excruciating pain. Do you have any idea how Zyklon B works?"

She is subdued, unfamiliar territory.

"No, I never..."

"The canisters fall to the floor of the gas chambers, the crystals form a gas on contact with air. It turns into Prussic Acid which passes through the mucous membranes and the skin, but principally through the lungs, into the blood. It blocks the process by which oxygen is released from red blood corpuscles and the result is a sort of internal asphyxiation. This is accompanied by symptoms of injury to the respiratory system, combined with a feeling of fear, dizziness and vomiting. That process of suffocation typically took fifteen minutes, fifteen minutes of agony. That's how my sister and my grandparents died. That is how millions died."

Delphine is sobbing gently.

"I'm sorry. I did not know. I had no idea that..."

Michael is relentless.

"And do you know why the Nazis used Zyklon B? Have you any idea?"

She shakes her head.

"Efficiency. It was the cheapest way to kill the largest number of people in the shortest time. The suffering of the victims did not make an iota of difference to the decision-making process."

She hesitates and then speaks impulsively.

"But if you, a Jew, abandon your God, does that not mean Hitler has won?"

He is white. His knuckles grip the table. He is trembling.

"First of all, I have not abandoned my God, or my people. OK I changed my name and that was because at the time I stupidly believed in the anti-Semitic myth of the rapacious Jew. But I never abandoned God. The tissues come out again. She supplies another batch and disposes of the soaking wad he gives her. She is anxious.

"Please. Please, I did not mean to... please, have some more wine, please."

He finishes his glass in one gulp. She frantically tries to change the subject.

"You have explained so much. So much that I did not know. This knowledge you have, about the gas and the way it worked. Please tell me that it has not destroyed you, made you hate all

Germans. What are your feelings about those who were born after the war had ended?"

"No I do not hate these young Germans, *maman*. I pity them. I pity them for two reasons. First because their generation will be reviled for what their parents and grandparents did. And second because many of them are still unwitting accomplices to the crimes of the Nazis."

"Accomplices? Surely not. The ones I have met are so opposed to the Nazi regime, so left-wing. Look at the Red Brigade."

"Well *maman,* over a million of the murdered Jews came from Germany itself, from Austria, Hungary, France, the Netherlands. How many carpets, how many dining room tables and chairs, how many necklaces and earrings does that represent? Where are they now, these objects, these 'things'? How many left-wing students and solid Christian Burghers, drink their tea from Jewish porcelain, eat off Jewish plates with Jewish cutlery, sleep in Jewish beds, Look at Jewish paintings, without knowing it?"

"But these goods were sold to Germans who had lost everything, whose houses had been bombed."

"No *maman*, from 1941 to 1945, there was a so-called 'Aryanisation' market in Hamburg. Jewish goods, from all over Europe. Department stores would send representatives, locals would queue round the block. Bargains you see. A bargain basement for all good Germans, not only those who had lost everything. This property still exists. It still corrupts the German soul. That's why I pity them. The sins of the fathers shall be punished to the third and fourth generation."

His voice has grown hoarse. Does he really believe this?

Paris, 3rd September 1965

Delphine is unusually severe.

"You dare to quote the Bible to me and yet you are so bitter. Can you not see that this anger of yours will destroy you?"

"You have been asking a lot of questions, *maman*. Well maybe you can answer some for me. First, why did I study German at school? Why did I choose it as soon as I had the option, and then continue with it right through to eighteen? Why did I read Nietsche, even Mein Kampfe? Tell me that."

Delphine cannot tell him what she really thinks. It would hurt too much.

"German is a great language. The poetry, the philosophical literature. I am sure you were intrigued by Freud and Meyerhof. That must have been so useful for an aspiring doctor, a *psychiatre*."

"The fact is, I have no idea and neither do you, *maman*. There's something else. Something which has troubled me for many years. You are an intelligent woman. You saved my life, risked your life saving me. You showed such a lack of regard for your own life. Why did the Jews fail to show that courage? Why did they go sheep-like to their deaths? Why did they not try to save themselves, why did they not resist? What were they thinking? That their God would emerge from the Heavens and protect them? That this was His divine will?"

Delphine pauses for a long time.

"I cannot answer your questions, Michel. I know that there were many Jews in the Resistance here in Paris, in France and elsewhere. I know that the Germans were fiendish in the way they tricked millions, that no-one could believe the facts even when they were given proof. But I cannot answer the question. You must meet someone I know, a good friend. He too is Jewish. He was a *resistant* during the war. He will help you. We will go back to the hotel. I will telephone him and arrange for you to see him. His name is Robert Leblanc. Maybe he will be able to talk with you this afternoon and we can meet later and speak of other things, more pleasant things."

CHAPTER 5
Paris, 3rd September 1965

Michael sits self-consciously in the forecourt of the Cafe de Flore surrounded by noisy traffic and noisier American teenagers. Girls in shameless hot pants and mini skirts. Androgynous youths with their long hair and tight jeans. Loud, confident, arrogant. The exact opposite of him. They are poring over guide-books and exchanging wild claims in strident, harsh accents about the books they have read and the girls they have fucked. Were any of these brash young people a new Hemingway or Kerouac, or were they as vapid and superficial as they looked? Deep in the bowels of the cafe a young man with a pony tail wearing a holed sweater is obsessively reading a novel. His glass has been empty ever since Michael arrived, twenty five minutes at least, none of the waiters bother him. The next Sartre or Camus perhaps? The tables on the terrace are tiny and wobbly, the chairs, faded green wicker. The waiters aggressively homosexual. He has an unworthy thought. Probably all this has been done to make it more authentic. Still, an unlikely place to arrange a meeting. Perhaps this Robert Leblanc, what a cliché for a Frenchman's name, perhaps Robert thought it would be convenient for him. It was only a short walk from Delphine's hotel.

Robert had given careful instructions. Michael was to sit on the right side of the terrace, but was that the right side looking in, or looking out from the interior? He had forgotten to ask. He was to be reading a copy of The Times open at the editorial page. He feels like the heavy in some slick spy film. Wait, someone is coming. A tall man, about thirty five, tanned, dark-eyed, handsome, in polo shirt and faded tweed jacket, hair sleeked back. Mexican moustache sprouting a smoking Gauloise. His face is open, suave, urbane. A ladies' man.

He sits down and extends his hand.

"Robert Leblanc."

Classic French handshake. It is as if he is wringing out a small towel. Heavy accent, deep, husky voice.

"So this is the famous Michel. *Sa petite mascotte.* Delighted. I have heard so much about you over the years. Your antics as a child."

Robert's legs won't fit under the table. He splays them to the side.

"But of course you are now very different…"

Michael does not want to hear yet again that he is troubled. He interrupts.

"So you knew Delphine during the war?"

"No, no, I met her in forty seven, after they… after you had gone to England. She still talked about the pain of that separation more than a year later. Such despair. She is a very, how you say, remarkable woman. I am sure you know that."

"Well, saving my life was pretty remarkable, I only met her earlier today after eighteen years so. But yes, she does seem very special."

Robert's eyes have misted slightly. Is there real feeling there?

"So charming, such intelligence, a powerful woman who can be funny, someone who knows how to flirt. I propose to her at least once a week. Hey, maybe you could persuade her for me?"

Robert is smiling. Surely this is not a serious request. Michael decides it is a joke, sardonic French humour perhaps.

"I may propose to her myself if she is all you say she is. But she must be rich of course."

Michael has passed the test. Robert throws his head back and laughs long and hard. Michael, always on duty, notices a dark raised spot on his forehead. A melanoma perhaps. Should he say something?

A beautiful girl glistens past them. Robert looks appreciatively at her and smiles. She half-smiles back.

"Ah women. Such pleasure. Do you have anything like that in London Michel, any creatures quite so exquisite?"

Michael feels the prickles of sweat return to his palms. He puts his hands in his pockets.

"Well, maybe not quite so exotic. But we have beautiful girls."

"Of course, the English Rose...but they are frigid, no?"

"I don't like to stereotype anyone, Robert, I don't suppose you'd be too happy if I started talking about frogs' legs.

"Frogs' thighs Michel, *cuisses de grenouilles,* a *cuisse* is a thigh, not a leg..."

"...Frogs' thighs then. Do Frenchmen eat them all the time?"

"*Touché.* I deserved that Michel. You are right of course. I was not serious. But you are serious, perhaps too serious, *n'est-ce pas?*"

So intrusive, these French. Have they no sensitivity?

"Well, I have learned a great deal in a very short time. I thought I had succeeded in putting my past behind me. Now..."

"Look Michel, you are the professional. But it seems to me that the pain you felt as a young child has not diminished however much you try to cover it up. I imagine that your teenage years were pretty hard. Let's face it, we all need to find a new identity as we grow up, when we get to, what? Fifteen? Sixteen? We all need to, how you say, react against the values which have been imposed on us. You will have reacted more violently than others because of what had happened to you when you were young. As for me, my father was a little man. Horrified that I wanted to stay in Paris in 1940 and put myself at risk. Left me with my uncles to fend for ourselves. Ran away to the south. That's when I learned to despise him. But this phenomenon is not just me and you. Every teenager needs something new to believe in. Is this not part of what we all do when we, when we...what is the English expression?"

"Flee the nest."

"Exact."

The hands prickle again. Michael rubs them surreptitiously. Robert is used to this kind of reaction.

"I see I have ... how do you say... found a bit of your past? Something not very nice."

"Yes, yes you are right. I did have some very unpleasant memories. I was trapped in a world I detested."

Robert leans forward.

"So Michel, to more important things...Delphine has been telling me that you have a question?"

"Yes, well Delphine thought that you might be able to help me with a perception that has troubled me for years, many years."

"*Allez.*"

"I was always led to believe that most of the Jews simply accepted their fate, went sheep-like to their deaths."

Robert has become serious, almost tense.

Paris, 3rd September 1965

"Before I answer your question, Michel tell me this. Do you remember where you were, how old you were, when you first heard what happened, when first knew about the Holocaust?"

It is his first Christmas. His new parents have promised him a treat, 'Snow White and the Seven Dwarves'. A film *maman* had taken him to see in Paris. He is so excited. The cinema is full of noisy children, he is licking an ice-cream. The organ stops playing and descends into the ground like magic. The curtains open. Music, a cockerel crows, British Movietone News. The deep English voice, a loud voice he does not understand. Cars flit by. Someone in a waistcoat makes a long speech. The scene changes. Sad music, sad voice, bulldozers pushing strange piles of white stick-like objects into open ditches. What are they pushing? His new mother is crying, his new father is carrying him out of the cinema, hiding Michael's eyes as he sidles awkwardly past irritated children. Did Michael sense anything then? Did he feel that these piles of 'things' were bodies? That they were somehow connected to him, to his people?

"I'm not sure, Robert. I may have seen a newsreel about Belsen soon after I came to England. But it was much later when I really found out. I think my, my new parents tried to shield me from it all. I wasn't allowed to go to the cinema until I was ten. There was nothing at school, nothing. Only a talk from our Headmaster about anti-Semitism and how evil it was, after one of the Jewish kids had been bullied and called names."

Robert lights another Gauloise,

"So, where shall we start? You know about the Warsaw Ghetto of course?"

Michael nods.

"A bit."

"Tell me what you know."

"I know that the Jews fought with a few improvised guns and Molotov cocktails against regular troops and held them at bay for weeks."

"Is that it?"

Robert waits allowing Michael's embarrassment to grow and then a torrent of facts pour out.

"A few hundred Jews resisted the German army for over 30 days. The Jews had only pistols, improvised explosive devices and Molotov cocktails. The Germans had heavy guns and unlimited supplies of ammunition. Hundreds of Germans were killed in the fighting, many of them front-line troops. In the end, the only way the Germans could kill the Jews hiding in the cellars was by setting fire to building after building and then using various means, probably even poison gas, to flush them out. There was one other casualty, a London-based Polish Jew who committed suicide in protest at the failure of the Allies to help the Jews in the ghetto while this was going on. How much of this is new to you?"

Michael flushes.

"All of it, all of it."

"Shall I go on?"

"Yes, yes please."

"There was a huge escape from Sobibor. So successful that the Germans erased all trace of the camp there. There was a major revolt and escape attempt at Auschwitz. Then there were the partisans, the resistance, so many of us fought here in France. There were Jews leading groups in Italy, Holland and Greece, in the forests of Belorussia. But there were other acts of heroism. A young Lithuanian woman overpowered a Ukrainian guard and killed him on her way into the gas chamber. The Jews of Grodno fought back with sticks and knives when they were being herded to the gas."

Grodno, the name sears Michael's brain. The rabbi of Grodno. His grandfather. Robert does not notice the reaction. He presses on.

"And what of the thousands who went... as you would call it, 'quietly'? How many of them were tricked into believing that they were simply going to have a shower. Some people simply couldn't believe that Germans could be so barbaric. And when they were on those trains? What then? They had to endure a journey lasting several days without food and water, watching people die around them. When they emerged weakened and disorientated to the lights, the barking of the vicious dogs, the shouting. They had no idea what would happen. And you know, even if some of them did know and just walked in to the gas chamber holding a child, staying calm for the sake of others, that in itself was an act of courage, great courage."

Robert sips his coffee and stubs out his Gauloise. His flow is spent.

Michael feels sick. This is a whole other world. Jews prepared to die, to endure torture simply in order to...to what? To vindicate their lives, their identity. To proclaim their race. Why had no-one never told him this before? Why had his parents allowed him to believe that there was no resistance? How would this information have changed him? Would it have made him any more of a man? Any less ashamed of his people? Any less ready to abandon them?

Robert smiles grimly.

"You know Michel, we Jews, we all carry the Holocaust within us. Those images of Jews going into trains, lining up to be shot meekly in front of ditches, of naked women running towards their death. That is us. That is you and me. We are still part of that story."

Michael is shocked.

"Even if we escaped?"

"We did not escape. No-one really escaped. We are all affected, all of us."

He paused and dragged on his Gauloise.

"Look Michel, identity is not something which happens between people, it also happens within people. Those images make up one of the many identities we carry within us. You for example..."

"Me?"

"You, the perpetual victim, the cringing Jew..."

Michael has a memory of an eminent German Professor of Psychiatry who gave a lecture at his hospital, of his fawning servility when he asked his question.

"...the curer of sick people, the child of Delphine, the would-be Nazi."

"Never. Never that."

"Are you so sure? I can see that in myself."

"... the denier of your nation."

A flash of recognition. Robert lights another Gauloise.

"You know, we are not so different you and I, Michel. You think that Robert Leblanc is any more of a Jewish name than Michael Turner?"

"You changed your name, too."

"It was changed for me. From Leibowicz to Leblanc. That way I didn't have to change any of my shirts."

Robert laughs. A hollow, shamed laugh,

"Yes, I too was a self-hating Jew. Just like you. Maybe even worse than you. I should have been proud. I saw what the Germans could do. How ruthless they were. I knew how many of us Jews fought in the Resistance here in Paris, and all over the country. I did some errands for them myself after I turned fourteen. A few grenades, messages, guns at first. Nothing much. They gave me new papers, a new name. Got me a job as a delivery boy, for a *Charcuterie*, hiding their stuff in my *panier* under black market pork sausages. Perfect cover. Then later I got more involved, just for a few months, until Paris was liberated.

"The name the Resistance gave me, Robert Leblanc, the passport was a very good forgery. I just got used to it. The different reactions, the girls, it made everything so... Did tell someone once, a girl I was very...well, close to. She was horrified when I told her, said she thought she could always smell Jews, had a long shower and then left, three a.m. Me, I always prefer the easy option. So when the war ended, I just didn't go back to my real name. Besides it helped a lot in my job after the war."

"What was your job then?"

Robert fishes in his top pocket and flashes a badge.

"Still is. Policeman...Detective, second class Robert Leblanc of the *Surete* at your service. Joined the riot police, the CRS, with a few of the less radical guys from the resistance. The socialists were in power then. Police, Nazis, not so different, especially here in France. And yes, I see what you want to ask and the answer is that I knew what some of my colleagues had done. Still, I had to work with them. No point in rocking the boat."

"So that was it? Just... just expediency?"

Robert looks hard at Michael.

"For a long time, just that. It was only later that..."

Robert takes a handkerchief from his pocket and blows his nose. His face has reddened slightly.

"It was... they were coming back you see. From the camps, the factories, the internment. Haunted, terrified faces. Still emaciated. Can you imagine what it must have been like? You come back to your old home. Did this neighbour betray you to the Nazis? Was that butcher a collaborator? And the police? Well they...we were the worst. We had rounded them up, arrested them, pushed them into the holding camps, the cattle trucks. Done the Germans' work for them. I could see the sheer terror in their eyes as I walked past them. I was still in uniform then."

"And your...colleagues, Robert, how did they react?"

Robert fumbles with a Gauloise packet and drops his cigarette. His hand is shaking slightly.

"Oh, you know, everyone was very careful. I think some of them guessed about me. No-one said anything. Wait, there was one incident. '*Sale Juif*' or something like that. Not to me of course, never to me. Someone trying to get a permit to set up a clothes stall I think. Did I say anything? No Michael I did not. I let it go. He was my superior. You know how it is."

Paris, 3rd September 1965

Michael remembers the formal lunch at Medical School. The anti-Semitic joke. The laughter. His laughter.

"So what happened?"

Robert's hands are shaking more violently now. He makes three attempts to light another Gauloise and fails. He is staring into some dark void.

"A man. A tiny man. Half my height. I had been given a tip-off that there was a pick-pocket in the area. He looked so guilty, tried to slink away as I passed him. So I stopped him. He was cringing. His eyes darting everywhere. He had a small bag, a briefcase. I asked him to show me what was in it and he just went for me. Attacked me. No provocation. Starting trying to kick me and run away. Screaming something I couldn't understand. Something in what sounded like German. We were well trained. It only took a minute to get him in an arm lock. He started to cry pitifully, like a child, crying and babbling. I couldn't understand him at first. Then I recognised one of the words, *'Gaz'*. He was saying *'Gaz'*. I listened more carefully. His words. I will never forget them. *'Schlep mir nicht zum gaz. Schlep mir nicht zum gaz.'* I cradled him in my arms and stroked his bald head. Me! I kept telling him it was alright. He wasn't in Germany now. He was in France, in France. Then I was crying too. He was astonished. Then he realised. He pointed at me and said *'Unserer?'*

"One of us?"

"One of us. A Jew. I was nodding my head. Still cradling him, stroking him. I took him back to my flat and put him to bed. He hadn't slept in a room on his own for years. Then I heard his story. He'd been a chiropodist here in Paris. When he finally got back they gave him papers and told him to return to his *cabinet,* his practice. But the people who had taken it over refused to leave. Didn't think it was fair. Claimed they had bought it in good faith. Screamed at him. Kicked him out. That's when I met him. That afternoon. Can you imagine? First them, then me."

Robert's hands have stopped shaking. He lights another Gauloise and takes a long puff.

"Through Shimon, I met a lot of them. They all had a story to tell. And what stories? That's when I got interested. Wanted to know as much as I could about him and his friends. The Jews who came back."

Robert leans forward, a new intensity gravels his voice.

"And there was something else they taught me. Something much more important. The great lie which has followed us since the beginning of history. The idea that there is such a thing as a Jewish race."

"But surely this is what the rabbis want us to believe. That we are the seed of Abraham? God's chosen people?"

"People Michel, people. God's chosen people. Not a race, a people. Take me. My father was from Poland. A typical Yid, frightened of his own shadow. My mother originally came from a Berber village in the Atlas mountains of Morocco. Berbers were... still are...dark-skinned, straight-backed, proud. The Jews who lived among them settled there well before Christ. Even after the coming of Islam they were the same in everything except worship. They even called one another cousins, lived in the same villages. The only thing my parents had in common was physical attraction, and that didn't last long!"

Paris, 3rd September 1965

Robert stubs out his cigarette viciously.

"She was living in Marseilles. Her family had only been there a few weeks. She had just got a job as a receptionist at the company he worked for. He always used to say that the first thing he noticed was the Star of David around her neck and the second was her huge dark eyes."

"OK, Robert, so they were different. But does that mean they were not members of the same race?"

"There is no racial purity for Jews, Michel, especially not for Jews. Look at the pictures of snub-nosed, blond-haired Israelis, of Indian Jews, of Chinese Jews, of Ethiopian and Yemenite Jews, then tell me that there's any kind of racial link between them."

Michael shakes his head. This is too much to absorb. Had he spent all those years hating himself, his family, his 'special' race, the 'Chosen People', without understanding what the word 'Jew' even meant? He sips his *citron presse*. Not a race. Not a race. Of course. Whole nations which had converted to Judaism. So much intermarriage during pre-Roman times, so many pogroms, so many rapes, so many differences. Ashkenazi Jews, Sephardi Jews...

He feels drained, defeated. He had lived a lie. Hitler's lie.

"Yes Michel, Shimon taught me so much, so much about myself."

"And after Shimon, after meeting his friends, did you tell your colleagues you were Jewish?"

Robert tries to hide his shame.

"No. I just let things slide. Oh they probably know by now. Mmm, yes I'm sure most of them will have guessed by now."

Robert grins, a sheepish, self-deprecating, crooked smile. He spreads his hands.

"*C'est comme ca.*"

He looks away. His eyes clouded.

"Tell me Michel, from your training, what do you know of anger, anger at yourself which is not expressed, not managed? What happens to it?"

"You will experience it as self-hatred, Robert. It will prevent you from achieving any form of inner harmony, any peace. You will never be truly at ease, truly happy. You will be unable to form lasting relationships."

"So what is the answer?"

"The textbook answer is. Face it, go for honesty and not self-deception."

Robert looks directly at him.

"And loathing? Loathing for these so called victims, for other Jews? For yourself as a victim? Do you recognise that?"

Michael is back in his past again. An eighteen year-old screaming 'I hate you! I hate you!' at two distraught, contorted faces. The parents he had worn down with his constant 'logical' arguments. He had always thought he understood why he left home as soon as he could. Now the lines are blurred.

Robert is distracted for a moment, looking at two girls who have arranged themselves ostentatiously at the next table and ordered Pernod.

He pauses, lights another Gauloise and smiles at them. They giggle.

Paris, 3rd September 1965

"OK, enough of this. Let's talk about action. Now you know that Jews did fight back, that they were prepared to die, to be tortured rather than submit passively. In the right place, at the right time, you could have been one of those Jews. And it is not too late."

"Are you talking about Israel? I tried that, spent a few weeks there. They are not Jews, not Jewish, not like us. I stayed with a couple of people of my age for two days. Then instead of telling me to go, they got me completely drunk on disgusting Israeli Brandy and turned me out on the streets with my suitcase at one in the morning. I ended up lying on a bench vomiting for the rest of the night. I have nothing in common with those people."

"You can't judge a country, a whole ideology, just because a couple of teenagers behaved like shits. So what else is worrying you?"

"Their Jewishness is not like mine. Those people have a different way of behaving to one another. They're more direct, I just don't feel comfortable with it."

"A lot of 'those people' Michel, are the children of survivors, just like you. But they have been hardened. You have been made soft. Maybe you feel too insecure to survive there among people who know, really know, who they are? People without our neuroses."

The remark strikes at the pit of Michael's stomach. Robert is right of course, but to hear the words spoken...

"Look Michel, you are not the only one. I can't fit in there either. OK, so we need to think of some other way, some way you can regain a sense of pride, your understanding of who you really are."

Michael remembers Mathilde's words when she showed him her scars. 'The SS doctors took me one day. Injections. For some research project. The pharmaceutical companies who paid for the experiments wouldn't tell us what had been used, wouldn't even admit they had done wrong. Why? Why? The war was over. The Jews had survived.

"My aunt, Mathilde, the one who saved me. They did these experiments on her. The SS doctors injected her with some toxins which affected her badly. She has survived somehow, but she is in terrible pain and unable to leave her bed. The pharmaceutical companies deny that they were involved. I would like to avenge these obscene acts."

Robert produces a classic policeman's notebook and pen.

"Name?"

"Mathilde Beatrice Auslander"

"Concentration camp Number?"

Damn, why didn't he take a note of that?

"Sorry Robert, I will have to get that for you. I have a letter from her which should help."

"Let me see what I can do without it. Which camp was this and when did it happen?"

"Dachau between 1942 and the end of 1944."

"Right Michel. Give me a few days. I will find out what I can. I have friends, colleagues in Hamburg. The Germans were so efficient. There will be a list of the doctors who worked at Dachau at that time. Maybe even photographs and resumes. If we are lucky they may have published the results of their experiments in some journal or presented them at a medical conference of the time. I have heard of such things."

"Do you think your informants might be able to tell me where these doctors are now?"

"Possibly. I don't know."

Robert pauses.

"And if I find these people for you, what do you plan to do with this information?"

"I have absolutely no idea. Something. Something significant."

"Right, I will help. Do you read German?"

"Yes, 'studied it for years."

Robert's voice has changed. A defined, active tone.

"OK, I'll do it, but I must warn you. This vengeance you seek. It will change you. Whether you succeed or not, it will change you. Are you prepared for that?"

A new sensation. He will finally deal with this injustice. He will eliminate his shame.

"Yes. Yes I am prepared for that. For anything."

"And your career, your medical studies?"

"I have some time off quite soon. I have done my final examinations and will not know which hospital I have to go to for a while."

"OK, you will get your information. I have contacts, many contacts. This will not be hard. I will give the information to Delphine. She will send it on to you."

Robert stretches his legs, knocking the neighbouring table. The girls giggle again and smile back at him.

"Well Michel, I feel that we have achieved a great deal. It was also useful for me, you know. I have never told anyone about Shimon before today. I have never admitted that I hid my Jewishness...that I am still hiding it. I also feel, how you say, purged. If you resolve these matters, perhaps you will find some peace."

He pauses.

"OK, that's enough of the serious stuff..."

He motions with his head towards two French girls who have started glancing at them and whispering. Typically Parisienne, the allure they cultivate almost from birth.

"...Now let's have some fun."

He turns to them.

"Est-ce que je peux offrir un verre de Champagne pour celebrer votre beaute Mesdemoiselles?"

The two girls have been waiting for this. They pick up their bags and wriggle ostentatiously towards them, sitting down instantly in predetermined places. They had obviously chosen their prey some time ago. The taller of the two moves her chair very close to Robert's. The other is less obvious, but her eyes say a great deal.

Michael is completely out of his depth. His forehead moistens, his hands flap. He knocks over his glass of citron presse.

"Great idea Robert, I'd love to, really. But I have to get going. Late you see. Late for an appointment with Delphine, promised I'd...."

Robert stands. The eyes are hard. Again the rag-wringing handshake.

"Still some way to go then, I see Michel. *Tant pis*, Have a pleasant evening."

Michael turns slowly and walks away into his own humiliation.

* * *

Paris, 3rd September 1965

Humiliation. Hunched shoulders. Crunched, pocketed hands. Tensed neck. Pained ego. He wanders towards the River, past kerbside tables groaning with food and laughter. Past couples leaning into one another. Past a world he has never known. He struggles to distil the maelstrom of the day. Madame Gautier, the letter. 'I never replied.' Delphine, getting in touch with those poisonous feelings he thought he'd left behind. Her horror at his betrayal of... of what? An anachronism? Or was it that he had thwarted her attempt to save a member of the Jewish race, to raise one more real Jew? Was she right? If he no longer believed in the 'One True God' had Hitler really succeeded? Should he join a synagogue, wear a skull-cap, change his name back to Rosenberg, just to make sure that Hitler had not won?

Impossible. Why? Because he was still a coward. Still insecure. Still terrified by the same personal demons. Still cowering in the ghetto of his memories. Still oppressed by an event which ended over twenty years ago. Hide, keep your head down, don't make waves. How many times had he denied his race? How many times had he let a chance remark slide by, hardly registering his own betrayal? How many times had he cursed the fact that he had been born with a tiny turned-up nose?

And Robert? Larger than life, Hollywood Robert Leblanc? Detective Leblanc of the Surete? Robert who made him understand so much. Not a race, a people. Not cowards, brave men. Not one identity within us, but several. The Israelis, not softened by their pain, but strengthened by it. Even the little that Robert had told him of his own life seemed so impossible to grasp. Robert who still worked with people who had beaten Jews and sent them to the camps, who had ransacked their homes. Robert, who still hid his Jewish identity from his colleagues. Should he be forgiven? They were the same, he and Robert, the same. Perhaps this vengeance will help them both?

A thought shocks him. Delphine. He had learned more about Robert's life than Delphine's. He knew nothing about the time she took him in. Her suffering when he was taken away, her life after he had gone. He looks at his watch. It is already nine. He turns and runs back through the crowds to the Hotel de Buci.

Delphine appears like a magician's assistant from the clunking, toy lift. She is flushed, tipsy perhaps. She is having trouble controlling her... her what? Her laughter? Is she laughing at him? Did Robert tell her what had happened at the cafe with the girls?

She senses his discomfiture.

"*Oh mon petit* is upset. Why?"

"It's nothing really."

"I am laughing while you look so miserable. You wish to know why I cannot share your angst. I have just been speaking on the phone to a friend, an Englishman, Alan. We have this little game you see. Invent phrases which are halfway between French and English – silly things. They always make me laugh. But it's just a silly schoolboy joke. It would not interest you."

So she thinks he is too serious to enjoy schoolboy jokes.

"No really, *maman*, I'd like to hear it. I like that sort of thing."

"Well he just invented the English for a *bateau mouche*. He decided it would be 'fly swatter', that's all. It doesn't sound so funny when you just say it like that."

"Sorry *maman*, I can't remember what a *bateau mouche* is. Should I know?"

Delphine is embarrassed. She colours slightly.

"There's absolutely no reason why you should remember what a *bateau mouche* is Michel. I apologise. I should never have mentioned it."

"Wait a minute, *maman*, *bateau Mouche*. I remember it now. Of course, the boats on the Seine. So Bat...*aux Mouches* is Swatter of Flies."

He grins ruefully.

"That's a terrible joke!"

"At last, mon petit I see you can smile. Do you know that is the first time I have seen your...your, what do you call them, the little creases each side of your mouth?"

"Dimples?"

"Your dimples. They are the same...the same. I knew they were there of course. They were always there when you were tiny, except at bed time. Always there. I was beginning to think that life had washed them away. I am so pleased I saw them again...so pleased. Come, we will go to my favourite cafe...talk some more."

The conversation is light, inconsequential. She deliberately ducks all his questions about her life. 'I am not proud of what I had become.' She refuses to describe their early life together or what had happened when he was taken.

"Too painful, all that stuff. We have both been through quite enough for one day. Let's discuss...but what? I know... cinema, French cinema, *La Nouvelle Vague*."

Within seconds they are arguing over the final scene in *A Bout de Souffle,*

"Far too long, *maman,* as a doctor I know Belmondo wouldn't have been able to keep running like that."

"But that's the whole point, he is a man who simply cannot die. He is too substantial. Too full of the life force, and anyway it was a reference to Waydja's *Kanal"*

The acting in *Hiroshima mon Amour',*

"So wooden, and the girl was so irritating, why couldn't she just make up her mind?"

"A typical male response, Michel. Her pain was palpable. Her suffering was based in the guilt of the survivor."

The plot of *Les Quatre Cent Coups,*

"Did Antoine's mother have to have a lover Delphine? Surely that was a step too far."

"But it was a true story, Michel. You don't distort the facts in a true story."

Delphine orders a second bottle of vintage rouge. The time passes quickly. Finally they stroll back arm in arm. Michael gives a deep sigh. She looks at him.

"I understand...I understand completely. I see what we have been missing, *mon petit.* We have lost so much time."

"Well, we'll have to do something about that, won't we Del... *maman?"*

"When are you leaving?"

"The train leaves from the Gare du Nord at 9.30 tomorrow morning."

"She clutches his arm more tightly.

"So soon?"

"I will be back *maman,* I promise. As soon as I can get some leave from the hospital. I will come back and see you."

"And your address?"

"Here."

He has already prepared the details. She takes the paper and hugs him.

"I will miss you, *ma petite mascotte.* I am already missing you."

In the taxi back to his hotel he realises that Delphine had paid for everything, that he had not even offered once. He will make it up to her. She must come to London soon. He will send her a ticket.

CHAPTER 6
London, 6*th* September 1965

Delphine's letter takes only two days.

> *My Dear Michel,*
>
> *I have been overwhelmed with feeling since last week. It is so far beyond anything I could have wished for that we have found one another again at last.*
>
> *We seem to have so many points of compatibility. It is ironic, don't you think, that we could have felt so differently towards one another if you had stayed here in France for those twenty lost years. I don't believe that I would have endured your petulant, adolescent moods very well. That could have made us enemies, or at least, a more 'conventional' mother and son.*
>
> *I am sorry. This letter is sounding so stilted. It is my poor English and not the way that I am feeling about you. Writing to you, trying to formulate the English sentences, is so different from the intensity of the few hours we had together, from the sensation of seeing you, of being able to express my feelings towards you...and even of being able to tease you just a little bit.*

Thank you so much for the ticket. I have booked a room at the Baker Street Hotel for next week. So very quintessentially English, do you not agree? Conan Doyle with his fake spiritualism and his fertile brain. Even the name 'Sir Arthur' conjures images of Knights and Round Tables.

I know that you are very busy, so I will arrive early next Saturday morning and depart on Monday morning. I do hope that you will be free for the weekend.

There is another reason for my visit. I wish so much to pay my respects to your aunt, the woman who had such courage.

I have attached Robert's letter about the SS doctors who did the experiments. I am not clear why this is so important to you. When we meet, you must explain to me why you have embarked on this singular quest.

I am so excited by this new phase in our lives. I hope that it will help us both to make some sense of our past and lead us into new territory.

All my love to ma petite mascotte.

Your maman,
Delphine

London,6th September 1965

The other letter is more official. The stamp of the *Prefecture de Police*, *9e arrondissment*. Two stapled photographs, photocopies or faxes.

Dear Michel,

My colleagues in Hamburg came up with three names and some photographs. Two may still be alive, although neither of them can really be linked directly to the experiments which were performed on your aunt. But there may be something for you to go on.

No-one else seems to have survived...unless they are in South America of course. I apologise that there is so little information. However, there is one connection with the name Auslander. It may be of no relevance, but the wife of Dr. Walter Borrelle died a few months ago after a long period of depressive illness. She was in a mental hospital near Dortmund. Borrelle collected her body but refused to take any of her belongings. The single case she owned was turned over to the police because the clinic did not know what to do with it.

'The case contained some sort of journal which had the name 'Auslander et Cie' engraved in small lettering on the back cover. This could just be chance. There were many Auslanders in the camps. Please inform me if this may have belonged to a member of your family and you would like me to try and get this item for you. There will

have to be a very good justification for them to hand it over. The Germans haven't changed that much!

The first photograph is that of Dr. Franz Sterberbett. He studied in Munich from 1933 to 1940. He is from a very rich family. He only worked in the camps for a few months. His experiments included injecting toxins (gasoline etc) into patients. Apparently he worked with some pharmaceutical companies, so he might be your man. He was held briefly by the Allies and then released without charge (not that unusual in those crazy post-war years). After that he bought real estate, set up a clinic and practised medicine in Germany. But he dropped out of sight a few years ago and probably changed his name. No-one knows where he is now.

The other one is Walter Borrelle. He also studied at Munich and qualified in 1941. He is known to have performed low pressure experiments on Jews. He also froze young Polish officers to death in experiments for the Luftwaffe. There are records which show that he worked in Dachau for some time, then changed his identity and went to the Eastern Front. He was captured in late 45, tried for his crimes and sentenced to five years in prison. There is no record of him serving any of that prison sentence. He has been working in the General Hospital in Dortmund for several years, a low profile job. (To be near his wife's nursing home perhaps?) During the war he gave a paper to a conference about his work trying to

London,6th September 1965

save Luftwaffe pilots who were forced into high altitudes during dog fights. It seems that victims were locked in a chamber. The pressure was then lowered to the point which corresponded to the kinds of situations the pilots could face, such as freefalling without oxygen. Apparently, after the war, the Allies made use of this information for their own Airmen. A film was made of one of his experiments, you will need to use your initiative to get a copy, but your medical credentials will no doubt help. There is some evidence that he might have helped Sterberbett with the toxins experiments, but nothing conclusive.

The dead man was called Dieter Braunsch. Not much good to you really, but the name came up so I thought I'd put it in.

There is another source they gave me. But according to my sources it is less reliable. The owner of a shop in Geneva called 'The Mercenary'. He is called Vittorio Bruneschini. He sells military memorabilia to right-wing tourists. We believe that he has close links to Borrelle. But be careful, he could also be very dangerous. Do not tell him who you are. He is the enemy.

I wish you Bonne Chance with your project. You will have my full co-operation.

My Distinguished Salutations,
Robert

PS Thank you so much for telling Delphine about the spot on my forehead. It was removed last week! RL

He looks at the photographs. Walter Borrelle, a frontal view and profile on the same sheet. Completely bald, dishevelled eyes, troubled face, crumpled mouth. Stooped. Unmilitary. A man who has fallen from grace in his own eyes. Sterberbett is so different, a young officer in full SS regalia, a carefully arranged photograph, for his parents perhaps. His body is slightly turned so that the head is at an angle, a classic pose. Hair carefully combed. Wavy. Neat. The face looks directly into the lens. A long face, piercing eyes, cleft chin. A nerveless face. This is an idealist, a man who knows he is right. The malignancy is already there.

Was Sterberbett the man who injected the toxins into Mathilde's leg? Did Borrelle help him? That is not the issue. The only question for Michael is this: Did these men treat humans like laboratory apes? Did they ignore their suffering, their pain?

CHAPTER 7
London, 10th September 1965

The young man at the desk of the Baker Street Hotel is busy picking his nose and arguing with his girlfriend on the telephone when Michael arrives. It takes a full seven minutes before he slams the phone down and glares at Michael as if the argument has somehow been his fault.

"Good morning. I have an appointment with Madame Garrigue."

"No Garrick staying here mate."

"Garrigue is spelled G-A-R-R-I-G-U-E."

The youth consults the hotel register.

"French is she?"

"Yes... French."

"Oh yeah, Garrig-you, Room 42. Phone's over there."

Delphine materialises into the faded lobby. She blazes with presence, with self-possession. Michael had heard of Chanel of course, even seen TV news programmes of mannequins parading back and forth, poe-faced, like sulky greyhounds. But he had never seen the real thing. Straight blue-black jacket, tight skirt with wine-red, beaded edging. Severely cut, accentuating her delicate form. Still the *gamine* after all these years. Pill box hat over cropped hair and mascara-enhanced eyes. Only the worn shoes give evidence of her predicament.

Delphine gives a little twirl and grins broadly at Michael, almost girlish.

The porter gulps.

"*Maman*, you look so..."

"So French? And why do you think that might be, *ma petite mascotte?* Now give me *une grosse bise.* Both cheeks remember."

Michael complies, only too aware of the impact on the young man, who minutes ago had written him off as some minor solicitor's clerk.

"Come, *maman,* I have a taxi waiting. I'm taking you to my favourite place in all London. It's very near here, the centre of Regent's Park."

The Secret Garden in August had never let him down. How many girls had 'ooed' and 'aahed' at the magic of the place, imagined him more caring, more sensitive because he took them there? This time there is no pretence. This time he wants Delphine to see the real London, the London of parks and light, not the London of fogs and inhibitions.

The gate seems locked. A firm push and they are in a different dimension. A long arch of jasmine and ancient wisteria feathered by young pink rambling roses. On either side, narrow beds of fuscias. They emerge to a massive stone urn full of box topiary, turn a corner and find a silken lawn, assymetrical flower beds, lavender, asters, huge clusters of euphorbia, and, between the bushes, a mauve and white Persian carpet of cyclamen.

Delphine is entranced.

"So different from our formal blocks of colour, our rigid geometric patterns."

London, 10th September 1965

They pass an arch of honeysuckle, a circle of grafted espalier trees, bare and tortuous. Michael leads her to a bower, sprinkled with inconsistent sunshine. To a high-backed seat, simple, unadorned. Delphine closes her eyes and sighs.

"I have thought so much about our first meeting, the argument, everything, Michel. We have already found an intimacy, a way of being. And today I will tell you about myself, who I am. But first, there are two things which puzzle me. Two questions which have worried at me since our parting."

What is she going to ask him? He has already told her more than any other human being.

"I will try to answer *maman*. But..."

"...No Michel, I...I see now how much pain you are still guarding, I promise that I will not ask you to visit that dark place again."

She takes his hand.

"Tell me *mon cher*, your decision to become a doctor, was it a calling, a vocation?"

Michael is relieved.

"In a way, yes, *maman*, but it started many years ago when I was still very young. It's a long story."

"We have the time Michel, this is so important for me. Anything which will help me to understand you is most important."

"Ok. You remember what I told you about my English father?"

"Of course. An immaculate man with his jokes, his bow tie and his black suit."

"Yes. Well, he worked for an insurance company and that insurance company was very famous. It's called Prudential Assurance. Father was the 'man from the Pru'. One of thousands of agents they employed around the whole country. His job was to look after our community. They were clever, they knew that Jews would prefer to do business with other Jews."

"Ah, I understand now Michel, why he had so many friends, gave so many parties."

Michael smiles.

"Always happy. Always entertaining guests."

Michael's face clouds.

"I remember it so well. Early Thursday afternoon. Scored an own goal at soccer so no-one would speak to me on the way home. My satchel was heavy with homework, Physics and History.

"My dad was sitting there in the kitchen. No bow tie, no jacket, no smile, no welcome. His face was crumpled. Then I saw them, the tears. He was crying...crying and repeating the same thing. I couldn't make out was he was saying at first...something about an old boot. Then it was clear. 'Chucked me out like an old boot after twenty years. Twenty years without a word of warning.' "

"Ah *mon petit*, at last I see a little of what you were as a schoolboy. Your voice. Your mannerisms. You are 14 again... But what had happened? Had he been dismissed."

"They called it 'letting him go'. Some sort of restructuring. It had been his life. He didn't know who he was any more."

"And his wife?"

"Mother? Oh, she was hopeless. Completely out of her depth. She had never seen him like that, you see. Just ran to her sister down the road as soon as she saw what had happened to him. Couldn't cope. The crying went on for weeks. I would go and sit with him every day after school. Sit and play chess with him. We didn't talk much, just played game after game of chess. I sort of let him win, I think he knew. Then we started to talk, well actually I started to talk. Told him how much he meant to me, to his friends. Somehow I knew that I needed to speak very softly and gently. He started to take notice. The crying stopped. The next day I told him how much I loved his jokes..."

Michael pauses.

"...even tried to imitate his voice when I repeated my favourite ones back to him. That's the first time he really looked at me. There was a sort of a grin, not a real one, but he was trying to. So I thought of other things to say which would make him feel good about himself...mmm, yes, I remember now. I reminded him how he'd helped Mrs Levy and her three kids when her husband was killed in a car crash. How he'd persuaded the bank to give her a temporary loan and then got the insurance payout sent to her much quicker than usual. Told him how grateful she was. Then I read him the speech he had made at my Barmitzvah the year before. He was so touched that I'd kept a copy of it. I exaggerated all his gestures and pauses. He started to smile. By the end of my performance he was in hysterics. Made me read it again and again. The next day he was almost his old self again. It only took him a fortnight to get another job, all those loyal clients you see. About a month later he called me into the lounge. That was a very big thing. No-one ever went into the lounge, except when great grandma came. Pale green Chinese carpet, big, black grand piano, wine velvet sofas. Anyway, he was sitting there looking very serious. I wondered what I had done wrong. Thought he'd found out about me and Melvyn smoking his fags. But it wasn't that at all. He sat up very straight and sort of made a speech at me. Told me how I'd saved his life. He said I had a 'gift', a special gift of helping people and that it would be a crime to waste it. Said he knew that I would make a fantastic doctor, a real healer of men, that's the words he used, 'a real healer of men'. Promised he'd support me through medical school. Seven years. What could I say? I hadn't even thought about being a doctor before. But it did give me a kick to see how I'd been able to help him."

"At last Michel, you are beginning to be honest with me. Up until now I had the impression that you were, well, holding back some information."

Delphine reaches in her bag and dabs her nose with her tissues.

Michael reddens slightly. There is so much he has not told her. How his father had cried and begged him never to take up a job which would make him vulnerable to the kind of humiliation he himself had just suffered. How he'd used a swear-word for the first time in Michael's presence. 'Those bastards shat on me.' The blackmail. 'I see now why we took you in and gave you a good Jewish life, my son. You have repaid me a hundredfold. Now you can make sense of everything that has happened.'

They sit for a moment in silence. Delphine takes his hand.

"And afterwards, Michel, after he recovered, did things return to normal between your parents? Did she forgive him? Did they go back to their social life? Enjoy themselves as much as before?"

An image appears. Dad standing at the foot of the stairs, impeccable as ever. Waiting. Waiting. Waiting. His voice a half-whine.

'Roberta, we'll be late, they'll start to eat without us. Remember how angry David was last time!'

London, 10th September 1965

Pain behind dad's eyes. Pain because he knew that all her preening and primping and perming and pouting was no longer for him. Pain that his place had been taken, not by one single man, but by men in general. Pain that his wife's favours would be spread thickly and obviously.

And the pain deepened with time. Her blatant flirting with his friends and colleagues. Her unexplained absences. Her late night assignations. Then, the ultimate humiliation. Their wedding anniversary, a young man, a new face. How long did they disappear for? Ten minutes? Twenty minutes? Yes, dad was being punished. He would always be punished. Michael gazes for a few minutes at a sculpture half hidden by Cyclamen. A huge hand enclosing a small child.

"Well you know, *maman,* she was different. But they managed somehow. There was a change, a coolness between them."

Delphine stands and looks at the Cyclamen for a long moment. Then she comes back and sits.

"Now it is my turn to be honest, *mon petit.* I have been very selfish with you, stupidly trying to protect myself, and I have hurt you."

"No *maman,* you cannot hurt me. You could never hurt me."

Michael is disappointed. He had wanted the Secret Garden to be a magical place, a place without ghosts, without recriminations.

"You have a right to know everything about me, Michel. I should have told you in Paris. Now I am prepared. After all, you are a man now. You must know the truth about the woman who saved you. I am sure that you have been imagining so many things since Mathilde told you what I did for my...my profession."

Of course he had had thoughts, fantasies. But does he really want to hear the truth? Delphine sees his hesitation.

"No Michel, this is not unreasonable. Mathilde will have told you that I was a woman who had protectors...admirers. Who was always beautifully dressed. It is natural to make certain assumptions. But I must explain how I became... what had turned me into the person who took you in."

"You don't have to *maman*, really. It's OK. It will change nothing."

"I know. I know. But you see *mon petit*, I want to tell you. I need to tell you."

She smiles ruefully.

"Everyone knows the story of the country girl who comes to Paris to make a career in fashion, in modelling, and the..."

"...And the older man?"

"And the younger man. Younger than me but already married."

She pauses. Her eyes glaze.

"You have the same expression in English I think Michel, the '*coup de foudre*'?"

"Of course."

"Have you ever experienced anything like that?"

He blushes.

"No not really. I have never found..."

Delphine takes his hand. Does she sense his pain?

"You will, you are still young. It is a remarkable sensation when you are standing next to someone you have never met before, never spoken to, and you know for certain that he will become your lover."

"Should you really be telling me this, *maman*?"

"Why not? You are no longer a child. Breakfast at my usual cafe. Busy. Cafe crème and croissant, strictly against the modelling agency rules. I was already late when he came in. I looked a mess, hardly any make-up, a shift I wore when we needed to do quick changes, flat shoes."

"And you looked at one another?"

Delphine's eyes moisten, she smiles wanly.

"Do you know, I don't think we even saw one another, really saw. I mean, I could feel his heat. I could sense the attraction, it was tangible."

"So what did you say?"

"Nothing, not a word passed between us. We both knew that it would destroy the moment."

"What happened?"

"Neither of us went to work that day. He was waiting for me as I came out of the cafe. I knew he would be."

Delphine is in another world, a world of impulse, of passion. Her eyes shine, her colour rises.

"This must be painful for you."

She turns, surprised.

"Painful? Not at all. It was my first *grande aventure* perhaps my only *grande aventure*. Paul, his name was Paul, told me, you know, even before we made love that first time. Said he was married. A family thing, arranged by their parents. Some aristocratic and business connections. He never lied to me, not about that."

Delphine seems restless. They get up and start to walk towards the Regency palace at the end of the gardens. Ornate railings, immaculate stone pond, huge and circular, life size bronze crocodile placed for effect just above the surface of the water. Michael can sense that there is a tragic ending to this tale.

"So what happened?"

"Ah, what happened. Well, they already had a child, Dominique. Paul brought him a few times, when we went to the *Jardins du Luxembourg* or the *Tuileries*. He was a sweet boy, sad, but sweet. Three years old when I met him for the first time, long blond hair, like you. I never thought of that before. Yes, very like you."

Delphine pauses and takes his arm.

"But not a charmer. You were a charmer, and you knew it."

She smiles wanly.

"I think we both hoped that it would just burn itself out. 'Too hot not to cool down', ah those American songs – such lyrics! But it didn't, it went into a second year and a third. I slipped gently into the role of the classic 'mistress' waiting for a chance to see him. Sitting at home on weekends and bank holidays, dreading Christmas and New Year.

"And all that time, I could not look at another man. I think I must have given out some sort of aura. Very few people even tried. I was locked into the pain of my impossible situation. I loved him and hated what he had made me."

Michael takes her arm and they walk towards a sculpture of a morbid looking young woman holding a ewe, inscribed with the message, 'To all protectors of the defenceless'.

"But *maman*, couldn't he see how much he was hurting you?"

"Of course he could see. He despised himself for what had made of me. I saw what it was doing to him. I think that's why I started to lose weight. Me, can you imagine what I would look like if I lost weight!"

"Anorexia Nervosa?"

"Amora frustrata. I was ready to die for love of him."

"And your parents. When did they become aware that...?"

"Oh, they knew at once that something in me had changed. Thought it was growing up pains, the stress of the big city. Country people you see. Eventually my father came to visit me. Some pretext or other. Within hours everything had changed."

"They took you to a doctor?"

Delphine picks a strand of hair from her forehead and replaces it carefully.

"Took me straight to a special hospital in Lille. The doctors there had seen it all before. Immediately gave me a sleeping cure which lasted ten days. Ten days of being fed by a drip, being sedated every time I came round. Saved my life, I'm sure of that now."

"And Paul? Did he try to see you?"

Delphine needs to walk. They pass into a narrow part of the gardens bordered by small conifers.

"Oh, *le pauvre* didn't know where I was. Tried everything to contact me. Even drove to Albi, to my parents' house. They weren't there of course, they were in Lille waiting for me to wake up. So my Prince did not find his Sleeping Beauty."

Michael is relieved, wishful thinking perhaps.

"So that ended it."

"Oh *mon petit* Michel, how little you know of love. That's when we knew that we could not live without one another; that life apart was simply not worth it. He had hired a detective to watch my apartment day and night. He was in my bed within 20 minutes of my return to Paris. On the stroke of midnight he proposed to me, went on his knees, begged me to marry him. I agreed of course. Our love-making that night was the best it had ever been."

"He divorced his wife?"

"Now we get to the heart of the matter, Michel. He tried to tell her, tried so many times. As soon as he started she would scream and throw things and drive him out of the house. That went on for several months. Eventually I offered to go with him. I thought I could give him, how do you say it, moral courage. Maybe if she saw us together she would behave in a more civilised way. She was, after all, from one of the great families of France. If she saw what we meant to one another, she would relent, she would see that their marriage was over."

Michael is shocked.

"Isn't that just the slightest bit unusual, even for France, *maman?*"

"Bizarre, I agree, even by French standards. We were both a little mad by then."

Delphine stops in her tracks, she starts to sob, a piteous keening. This time it is Michael who supplies the tissues.

"It was terrible, so terrible. I had never seen them together you see, never seen what she could do to him, what power she had over him."

"You mean he just caved in?"

"Oh, he was brave enough at first. But she was...and you know, I do admire her for this. She was implacable. These aristocratic French women are used to getting their own way from the age of zero. They believe that it is a sort of divine right. She was calm and civilised. But with every word she spoke I watched my beloved Paul diminish. He seemed to...to what? To deflate like a Michelin

London, 10th September 1965

man. He paled, stammered, sweated. Yes *mon petit* you are not the only one. He became fawning, obsequious. It was horrible, horrible.

"Her position was quite clear. I can remember the words even now. 'If you attempt to leave me, I will ruin you and your family. You think I haven't known about your little slut all these years. You think I have not prepared for this moment. I will tell the authorities about the way your father's company keeps two sets of books and salts money away in Switzerland. I will give the press a list of the politicians you have bribed. Then I will take everything, every penny you have, and you will never see little Dominique again. Do you really think your relationship could survive that?' I still hear those words ringing in my ears. Do you really think your relationship could survive that?"

"But why would anyone want to stay with a man, sleep with a man she had blackmailed in this way, *maman*?"

"Why? Perhaps she knew him better than I. Perhaps my understanding was distorted by lust?"

"So did he at least take you home?"

"He called me a cab...I sat there in a state of such shock. It was so surreal, the whole experience. I thought I would wake up and find that none of it had actually happened. The next morning they found him dead at the foot of his apartment block."

Delphine, is gasping. Her breath has given out. The pain is too much. He leads her to a bench and lays her down using his jacket as a pillow. Slowly she regains equilibrium.

"Dead. Paul dead. And I could have saved him. If I had told him that none of this mattered, that we would go on as before, that I would gladly be his mistress. No-one would have minded. It was *de rigeur* at the time. Every successful businessman or politician had a mistress. Some of these women became very respected. But I said nothing, nothing!"

Michael takes control. He guides her back through the long bower of white jasmine and wisteria, across the road to the healing power of the Queen Mary Rose Garden. They wander round the triangular beds, kaleidoscopic colours, heady perfumes, quintessentially English nature.

"And afterwards *maman?*"

"The colour rises in Delphine's cheeks.

"Afterwards. I think I went a little bit insane. More than a little bit insane. Do you know I was even a *danseuse* at the *Folies Bergere* at one stage...just for a few months."

She pauses. Her eyes dim.

"And then I slipped into a different role. It was like a completely new wardrobe. New clothes. A new persona. Finally I became the person I was when you came into my life with your tears and your potato smell. And it was you Michel. You, who gave meaning to my existence. A sense that I could still do something worthwhile."

She thinks of those early days with her *petite mascotte.* Of his bewilderment. His pain. Her ability to soothe. The facility she had with stories. Stories which took him into a new world. A world of heroes and giants and dragons and happy endings.

By the time they are ready for lunch, she is the old Delphine again. Only the red rims around her eyes remain as a testament to her pain.

He takes her to an Italian restaurant on Marylebone Road. Tatty, but the best Tiramisu in London. Plastic tables, so impacted they have to ask people to move so that they can get through. Loud Neapolitan waiters who flirt outrageously with all the women and break into clichéd song at the slightest opportunity. But when Delphine reacts with haughty disdain to the crass advances of the manager, the atmosphere freezes, the songs subside.

They are given an uncomfortable table near the toilets. Delphine accepts the slight graciously.

"Let's go somewhere else *maman*."

"Certainly not Michel. No-one will bother us now. And at least this table is secluded."

She pauses and looks hard at him.

"Now, *mon cher*, it is your turn."

Michael looks puzzled.

"My second question. It is your turn to answer. This one special girl you mentioned in Paris, Michel. The one you would not tell me about earlier today."

Michael is horrified. How could she know?

"Do not look so shocked Michel. Earlier, when I asked you whether you had experienced anything like my *coup de foudre*, I sensed that maybe there was someone once. Someone special to you. Honesty, remember. It is your turn to be honest about your love affair. What was her name? Where did you meet?"

"She was a year above me at medical school. Used to help me to revise anatomy, my worst subject."

"The older woman. Was she already experienced?"

"Oh, *maman*, you are so naughty."

Delphine's eyes twinkle.

"Tell me... tell me everything, what happened?"

"It was wonderful at first. Up to that time I had always held something back, a small part of me. But with Juliet..."

Michael is swamped by memories. The trips to Rome and Budapest hitching and staying in hostels. The sun beating down on their naked bodies as they lay on his bed half-asleep and sated. The sounds she made, a frantic dove-like cooing, louder and louder. Her screams.

"She was so hungry *maman*, always so hungry. How could anyone give herself like that and not be in love, completely in love?"

"You were a virgin?"

Michael crimsons.

"Of course that must have affected the way I felt. Distorted my view of her."

Delphine sighs.

"The eternal dilemma, when does love die and lust take its place?"

"Or was it always simply lust, *maman*?"

"It is never simply lust. Never Michel. Unless you are an animal."

"But surely love is giving and lust is taking, *maman*?"

"If only it were that easy, Michel."

She looks at him for a long time.

"So you opened your heart?"

"Yes. I thought, really thought I was safe with her. A feeling I had not experienced."

"At least not since our time together, *mon petit*."

Yes, *maman,* since you. Since I lost you...What a fool I was? What a complete fool? Oh, it didn't take long, three or four months.

Then she started to dismantle my self-esteem. First it was my snoring, then my moustache."

The pasta arrives. The manager serves them himself with a great flourish. He grates the Parmesan and then, without asking, produces a huge pepper mill and starts to grind the spice furiously into each dish, until Delphine stops him with an abrupt, 'Basta!'

Michael waits for the man to be out of earshot.

"She forced me to shave my moustache off, said it looked odd. I loved that moustache. A week later she was complaining that my face was out of proportion, that I had a huge space between my nose and my upper lip. Then it was my posture."

Delphine is baffled.

"She seems damaged, this Juliet of yours. Something has happened to her in the past, *non?*"

"If only you had been there to advise me, *maman*! I found out later, much later. Her first love. He hit her. Finally left her, but only after he had brutalised her, made her hate all men."

"But these little insults, they would not mean much to you if you were so in love?"

"I hardly noticed them. The process she used was so subtle. The next thing was the flirting. Oh, nothing obvious, just a little giggle and showing a tiny sliver of pink tongue. Then a light touch on their hand. Just what she'd done with me when we first met."

"But something else happened Michel. Something serious, *n'est-ce pas?*"

Six of them are at dinner discussing the film they have just seen. He is holding forth, explaining how unrealistic the plot was. He remembers her words so well. 'Is it the film or your own dysfunctional childhood you're talking about here, Michael?' He remembers his cold fury. He hardly knew these people! He remembers the feeling of being trapped, being unable to make a scene.

"There may have been some remark she made. I honestly can't remember it now *maman*. Anyway, it wasn't enough to make me leave her. The sex..."

"Like a drug? Something which consumed both of you?"

"Yes, a drug, an addiction. Whatever crimes she had committed, she could always get me back. The softness of her lips just behind my left ear. Infallible."

"*Mon pauvre*. She was destroying you. But remember, she was also destroying herself. She did not want to leave you. She needed you, if only to prove she was capable of loving, of being loved."

"You are being too kind, *maman*. After six months there was someone else. She kept avoiding making plans. 'I'm busy,' that's all she said, 'I'm busy.' We both knew what it meant. The next day we would make love and it would be as good as ever, better than ever. But I was being eaten alive. One night when she had told me she was 'busy', I drove to her house and watched. I saw them come back. About eleven. I saw the light go on in her bedroom. I saw her come in and draw the curtains. I saw the shadows. The light go off. The next day, it was a Sunday, she rang me early. Could she come and have coffee? Our code for sex. She came. We made love. But for the first time, I couldn't lose myself. I was watching her, observing her. Was she thinking of him while she was with me? She looked at me. Looked straight at me while I was in her. I saw a solitary tear form in the corner of her eye. It was over. I was free."

London, 10th September 1965

Michael blows his nose on his serviette. He cannot not hide the pain.

"And since then, Michel?"

The Dali postcard burns a hole in his jacket pocket. Tigers, guns, a nude. A likeness which is far more powerful than any photograph he has of her. What was it called? 'One second before awakening' Perfect description...for him at least.

"Oh, I'm over her, completely. And there are plenty of opportunities for a young doctor. Plenty of nurses, physios, technicians, even some doctors. But it is too raw, too recent. I need time."

"I see that there is still much you cannot tell me, Michel."

"What do you mean?"

"Please, *mon cher*, I am very experienced in these matters. Very experienced. There is much you have not revealed...to spare me perhaps. But this *affaire*. It was destroyed, maybe for another reason, *non?*"

How can he tell her that Juliet had been desperate to marry him? How she had wept, pleaded with him in those first months, offered to convert to Judaism. How can he tell this to the gentile who had saved his life. He cannot say the words. The tissues come out again. This time he has an ample supply. A serpent wraps itself around his chest. He must leave this place. He rises.

"Please, Michel, I am not angry with you, only sad. One day perhaps you will be ready to tell me the rest of the story."

He pays the bill. He had forgotten to order the Tiramisu. They drive back to her hotel in silence. A long, resonant silence.

CHAPTER 8
London, 11th September 1965

The door of the Cameron House opens within seconds of his ring. Matron is standing there. She squeezes Delphine's hand warmly giving Michael a cursory 'Hello.' Perhaps she still blames him for what happened last time? Delphine and Matron chat effortlessly during the long walk to Mathilde's room. Yes, he is definitely being ignored.

Mathilde has arranged herself even more carefully than usual. She is wearing a new pink, angora bed-jacket. Her hair has been curled and primped to draw the eye away from the face, beneath the pancake and rouge, her face has taken on a new colour, a grey-yellow tinge. Her eyes are ringed with red. Was this the result of tears? Or is it the disease which ravages her?

This time Michael has worked out exactly what he is going to say. He recites as if he is making a speech on a school open day.

"Hello Mathilde. How nice to see you. As you can see, I didn't forget the flowers. We must keep up our little rituals, don't you agree?"

He extends the flowers. Mathilde ignores him completely. She is staring only at Delphine, at her healthy complexion, her body, her carefully constructed image.

"Let me introduce you to..."

Mathilde's venom takes them both by surprise.

"...I know perfectly well who she is."

Delphine does not extend her hand. Somehow she knows that she will be rebuffed. Michael tries to cover his confusion. He puts the flowers on a side-table and pulls up two chairs. Delphine sits and folds her legs. Michael hovers, then sits down nervously. There is a silence which extends beyond Michael's breaking point.

"So Mathilde, it's been some time. What? Nearly four weeks? Tell me, how are you?"

"Think I look worse do you? Come to watch me die, have you? A little bit of support wouldn't go amiss you know. How about, 'How well you're looking Mathilde.' 'I do like your new hairstyle Mathilde.' Is that a new jumper Mathilde?' But no, all you can do is remind me how ill I am. Perhaps you should leave. Both of you."

Delphine's voice is gentle but there is no mistaking her tone,

"*Ma chere* Mathilde. I am so sorry. I can see that we have come on a bad day."

"*Ma chere* Delphine, every day is a 'bad day'. Have you any idea what it means to be in excruciating agony day and night. To be woken by pain and nightmares? No, I thought not..."

She turns to Michael and addresses him directly.

"...Why have you come back? I told you not to. You are only making things worse, much worse, reminding me of what might have been."

Michael starts to rise. Delphine puts her arm on his shoulder. He subsides into the chair.

"Mathilde, please. I know you are suffering and you are right, I have no idea what that must be like, but it is hardly Michel's fault. Can you not see how fragile he has become?"

London, 11th September 1965

"Why should he be fragile? What has he been through? Nothing. Nothing. I thought I had saved him so that he could be someone. Do something with his life. He is nothing. He should be strong, proud, not a blushing *pleurnicheur,* a cry-baby."

"He is not a *pleurnicheur* Mathilde, just a rather intense young man."

"He is a baby, a miserable worm. A man without courage. I see it on him."

Delphine reacts at once.

"That is so unfair and untrue. I think you should apologise."

Mathilde's face is puce.

"How dare you tell me what I can say to my own flesh and blood!"

Delphine ignores matron's frantic signals.

"He may be your flesh and blood, but I changed his nappies, wiped his nose, nurtured him as my own for over four years. Does that mean nothing to you?"

Mathilde has lost control. The hands are waving again, the voice is hoarse, strident.

"'Nurtured him as your own'. At least you enjoyed him. At least you saw him grow and learn to skip, to ride a bike, to read, to write his name. I lost him before he could even tell me that he loved me. I lost my sister's love because of him, my own sister. Any minute now you will tell me that you risked your life for him."

"Look Mathilde, believe me, I am very, very sorry that you are suffering, but what you just said is unworthy of you."

"Unworthy? Why? It is the truth."

"None of this would have happened without you, Mathilde. You gave your body to that grubby lout to save him. So much more than me. So much more than me!"

She has taken Mathilde's hands in hers. She is kissing them. Within seconds the two women are weeping in one another's arms, stroking one another's hair, consoling one another wordlessly.

Michael turns this way and that in his attempt to shake off the huge wave of feeling which engulfs him. His body begins to rock backwards and forwards. He feels his distress as pain. Intense pain. Pain he cannot resolve. His being is weeping but his eyes are dry. He cannot let go. He must not let go. Delphine draws him into her arms, into Mathilde's arms. He is crying now, sobbing like a child, like the three year old snatched from his mother's arms, like the eight year old taken again from light into darkness. When did he ever cry like that before? They are holding one another, crying and laughing, crying and laughing. They cry for an eternity. Then Mathilde leans back and smiles serenely, a smile he has never seen. She is her old self again, seventeen again. The women start chattering like school-girls. A signal from Matron and Michael slips out of the room.

* * *

They are still gossiping when Michael returns, sparking off one anothers' memories.

"Old man Lebec who kept budgies on his balcony and was always losing one. Perfectly named for his hobby, *n'est-ce pas Mathilde?*"

"That boutique on the *Square du Cour,* Delphine. So cheap, so chic. Great, except for the dragon lady who would throw you out if you tried to bargain."

London, 11th September 1965

"The enormous *blanchisseuse* who sang exactly like Edith Piaf." They hardly hear him come into the room. He coughs apologetically and they both look up as if drawn by the same puppet string, glance briefly at one another, try their best to contain their mirth and then explode into gales of laughter.

Michael blushes and instantly looks down at his flies. Had he forgotten to zip himself up when he went to the toilet? They laugh again, even louder.

When they have recovered, Delphine takes pity on him. She embraces him gently.

"Mon pauvre petit. No, we are not laughing at you. We are laughing...well, because we have discovered one another and we are enjoying one another too much. We have become schoolgirls again.

Mathilde beckons to him warmly. He goes to her. She hugs him long and hard. Again he is reminded of her bird-like fragility.

"Your *maman* Delphine...yes she is really your *maman* now. She is such a special person. What instinct made me choose her above all others? A sign from somewhere. She is wonderful, wonderful."

She extends her hand. Delphine takes it and kisses it.

Mathilde is affected by this gesture. She becomes agitated. The hands have started fluttering, the voice breaking up. Matron appears and inclines her head imperceptibly. Michael rises and looks at Delphine.

"We must go now Mathilde."

Then he remembers.

"Mathilde, my darling Mathilde,"

Matron is signalling furiously.

"There is one question I must ask you before we go. Did you or my mother take anything with you when you were...arrested? A diary perhaps?"

Mathilde's hands have stopped.

"Not a diary, a journal."

"Can you describe it for me?"

Mathilde is frowning, remembering a long spent emotion.

"I was so jealous. *Papa* gave it to Augustine a few weeks before...before the end. He told her that, if the worst happened, she should write down everything she saw, keep a record so that the world would know what degradation the German nation had sunk to. I remember his words. He was so serious and I was so jealous."

"And what was it like, Mathilde? Can you describe it to me?"

"Black alligator skin journal. So beautiful, shining, elegant. An ornate clip, two gold alligator heads interlocking in a secret way. Why couldn't I have such a beautiful thing? I was always left out of it, the youngest. Not serious enough for *papa*. I remember the last hours in Pithiviers, packing for the transport, pleading with her to sell it for food. She would not give in. *Papa* had given it to her. She would keep a record of what she saw. She slipped it under her skirt to hide it from the guards. She even had it with her in the camp until she had to undress. Then they took it."

Michael cannot not contain his excitement. Matron is signalling furiously.

"And was there anything engraved on it?"

Mathilde shook her head.

"I am not sure. I think it was just the year. I still remember that wonderful shine. It seemed to give out a glow, even in the dark."

"Nothing at all?"

"Wait. Yes, there was the name of my father's bank. *Auslander et Cie,* on the back in very small letters. On the back, yes. In gold, very small. He had had them made for special clients and kept two for himself."

Michael turns to Delphine. She had never seen him look so determined.

"Maman, you must recount this conversation to Robert. Please ask him to do his best to find it."

Mathilde is leaning forward.

"You mean you know where it is? That you can get it?"

"I cannot be sure Mathilde, not yet. It may be difficult, but we will try, won't we Delphine?"

Delphine picks up on the nuance.

"Yes, we will try. We will do our best."

"You must. You must bring it to me. Augustine's journal. Augustine's journal after all these..."

Mathilde's eyes start to roll into the back of her head. She is unconscious.

Matron is reassuring.

"Don't worry, This is not serious, It has all been a little too much for her. She will sleep now. She will be alright tomorrow. Come back soon and bring the journal if you can, please. You can see how much it would mean to her."

They tiptoe out of the room.

*\ated**

          * * *

Michael's driving is erratic, frenetic. Delphine is barely conscious of the fitful stops and starts, the hooting cars. Awkwardness walls her into her own thoughts. Of course she had seen the grainy black and white film of corpse-like spectres, pyjamaed figures, grinning into the camera, the television interviews with tortured souls. But somehow that never really touched her. Here in Mathilde it is tangible. Mathilde, whose entire life had been distorted with pain and anger. Mathilde, the manifestation of that single word, *'Holocaust'*. Now, at last Delphine can begin to understand why finding Mathilde has made her Michel so ready to bleed. What can she say to this man, this boy?

Michael is still rotating on that one moment. The moment when his soul burst. The moment when his world changed for ever. Would it last, this freedom to feel, to express his feelings? Would he be able to cry again? Cry as he had in Delphine and Mathilde's arms. His eyes fill as he remembers.

They arrive in silence at Delphine's Hotel. He pulls into the curb and looks at her. Delphine moves to take his hand but stops, instinct telling her that he would recoil. The emotion is still too powerful. She sighs.

"I remember when you were three, Michel. I bought you a tricycle for your birthday. You were so excited, you jumped on it and tried to pedal. But for some reason you could only pedal backwards. The tricycle would not move. I tried holding your feet and pushing, but as soon as I let go, there you were pedalling backwards again. You were so frustrated. I told you that it did not matter, but you

London, 11th September 1965

were irreconcilable. I had never seen you so angry. But you would not give up. You sat on that tricycle and pedalled backwards for hours, you refused to eat for days. Then one morning, very early it was...about six o'clock, you came pedalling into my bedroom. You were laughing and crying with joy, just as you were today in my arms, in Mathilde's arms. You had conquered yourself. And you had achieved it all alone.

"When I looked at Mathilde today, when I saw the rage, the obstinacy, the refusal to give in, I saw something of that three year old boy. You have the same ability to overcome your obstacles, to succeed against the odds. That is what has taken you so far. That is what helped you get to where you are, despite your past. Many people would be debilitated by what you have been told of your mother's, your sister's murder. Destroyed by a sense of despair and impotence. But you Michel, I know you will be strong enough to cope with the information you have been given. You have the resources to use this part of your history, of your family's history in a positive way. To move forward. To exorcise these new demons."

Michael leans forward and embraces her.

"I will try *maman,* I will try. I promise."

"But now, *mon cher,* we must act. We must find your mother's journal. It will mean so much to Mathilde. Give her a new lease of life, make her strong again. This information Robert gave you, bring it with you tomorrow, perhaps I can make things go faster, get the journal myself."

They embrace. She walks slowly towards the hotel entrance, turns and mouths the words, *"A demain."* Then she disappears.

CHAPTER 9
London, 12th September 1965

Charing Cross, Monday morning. Trains spewing termite commuters, with their brollies, their bowlers and their vacant frowns. Rain. Cold. Classic, unseasonable London weather matches their mood.

They hurry down platform six looking for a less crowded compartment. They are late. Delphine would not leave until she had made sure that she looked superb. Michael is lugging her suitcase, limping with the bulk, the weight. He hated to be late. Hated it more than almost anything else. She kept him waiting in that dingy reception with that supercilious porter sneering behind his hand. Why? Why were women like that? Delphine broke the icy silence which had pervaded the taxi journey.

"Have you forgiven me?"

"Of course. It's one of my... my things...lateness, rushing."

"I know. I'm sorry."

She stops. Turns to him.

"This is going to get harder each time."

"Yes, but it is so... so ..."

"...So important, yes Michel, to us both."

A brief inaudible announcement. Stragglers are running down the platform. Delphine climbs aboard and stands at the entrance embracing him awkwardly. For the first time she is much taller than him. A sudden sense of the way his *maman* had once bent down and held him in her arms when he was four invades, then leaves him. He looks at her and marvels at her ability to look attractive even when her face is wet, her mascara smudged.

"Oh, I almost forgot, I have brought you the details which Robert sent me."

He hands her the addresses.

"It may not be so easy *maman*. These German authorities, can they really be made to cut corners, let it disappear?"

"Don't worry Michel, no-one really likes endless paperwork, not even the Germans. I will go and see them myself. I have her Concentration camp number and a copy of her French identity card. I promise that she will have her sister's journal. That is the least she deserves."

"Thank you *maman*. Thank you so much."

Her face is searching his.

"And you, Michel. What do you plan to do with the information, the details of these doctors?"

"I don't know *maman*. But something. I will do something."

"And if what you decide to do, changes you? Corrupts you?"

"I know that it will change me. But I need that. Now that I know what happened, I need to be changed. Trust me *maman*, I will be alright, I promise."

"Please, I beg you, *ma petite mascotte,* do not abandon the values I gave you. Do not let me down."

There is a second announcement. The train lurches twice and is gone.

* * *

London, 12th September 1965

Her letter arrives five days later, a Friday morning.

> *Mon cher Michel,*
>
> *I went straight to Germany from Calais and spoke directly to Robert's German colleagues. They seemed very amused at first, but they gave me the journal when I explained that it had been the property of a Holocaust victim. Actually, they seemed to want to get rid of it, and of me.*
>
> *The first few pages have been written on in German. A diary account of some kind with dates. There are smudges, tears I think. German, such a horrible language. I am so glad that I never learned it. As far as I can tell it is an educated woman's writing. Very neat and precise at the start. But towards the end, the writing changes. It is less ordered, as if the writer has become more emotional. I have posted the journal straight to Mathilde at the Nursing Home. She seemed so very keen to have a memento of her sister.*
>
> *Please telephone me and let me know Mathilde's reaction when you next see her.*
>
> *My salutations to ma petite mascotte from your regenerated maman.*
>
> *Delphine*

CHAPTER 10
London, 18th September 1965

The familiar ring insinuates itself into Michael's fitful dreams. What time is it? He checks his alarm clock. Three thirty. Is he on call? He gropes unsuccessfully for the phone. When he finally retrieves it from the floor, the line is dead. It rings again instantly. His voice is hoarse with sleep.

"Dr Michael Turner here. What's the emergency?"

"Dr Turner, my name is Sister McCarthy."

So it is the hospital. One of his patients perhaps? What has he done wrong? Who is this mealy mouthed, thin-voiced nurse? Why does he not know her?

"I am the chief night nurse at Cameron House. I understand that you are next of kin to Miss Mathilde Auslander."

Aunt Mathilde? His head is ice.

"Yes, yes, she is my aunt. What's happened? Is her illness worse?"

"Your aunt suffered a massive M.I. a short while ago."

Her voice is too dispassionate, too slow, too calm. How can she talk like that? How?

"According to Felicity Slewitt's notes, a package arrived from France by special delivery this afternoon. Mathilde was very excited at first but became very distressed when she read what was written. She was immediately given a powerful sedative, but the damage had been done. She slept only for an hour and woke screaming your name. A few minutes later, the heart attack occurred. We have a doctor on site and he has given her the appropriate medication. He is here now and wishes to speak to you."

A young voice. Thick with emotion.

"Dr Turner. I am Ezra Levi, house doctor here. I have done what I can, but your aunt has so many co-morbidities. She will not survive for much longer. I believe that she is hanging on to life in order to tell you something. How soon can you get here?"

"Twenty minutes."

"Very well. Please remember to ring the night bell. We are trying not to disturb the other residents. They get distressed by these...these events."

The journey from Muswell Hill is a blur of hooting cars. A thought intrudes. Was this the record for red lights crossed in the shortest time?

Cameron House looms. The winding path is treacherous in the dark. He rings the usual bell, the old bell pull – no sound. Then he remembers. The night bell, Levi said use the night bell. Where is the fucking night bell? He takes an age to locate it behind the Clematis. Sister McCarthy answers at once. She is small and pretty, an open, freckled face. But her voice is the same. Prissy, officious, emotionless.

"Come in Dr. Turner."

"How is she?"

"There is very little time."

They hurry down a dim corridor to a new wing. Of course there would have to be medical facilities here. A blast of light. They

London, 18th September 1965

turn into a blazing room. Doctor Levi is adjusting a drip. A nurse is recording vital signs.

Mathilde has shrunk, a barely visible huddle of blankets and tubes. Her once careful hair is greyly awry. Her face skeletal. Her eyes gather liquid fire when she sees him. The Oxygen mask obscures her face, but not her feelings. Her rage gurgles through the plastic. She tries to lift her head. Michael removes the mask. Her face is pale green. Perspiration feathers her forehead, her cheeks, her upper lip. She wants to say something. Nothing, only a hoarse impassioned croak. She throws off her blankets. Michael sees the body she has been at such pains to conceal. A hollowed out husk. The back, a framework of bones, the ribs caved in on themselves like a dismembered galleon. He gasps at the damage all those years of illness had done to her.

There is a glass of water and an envelope by her bed. Michael moistens a sponge and puts it to her lips. She sips and sucks urgently.

"It's alright now Mathilde. I am here. I will look after you. Your Michel is here. I will stay with you. I will not leave you."

She motions him impatiently towards the envelope. Her hoarse croak becomes articulate.

"Augustine's journal. It has been contaminated, sullied, defiled. Such words, such despicable, such abominable words. Delphine. What possessed her? How could she...? You must promise me something."

Her hand clutches at his. The grip is iron.

"Do you promise? Do you?"

"Yes, Mathilde, I promise."

"Promise you will destroy this evil, obscene thing."

"I promise. Mathilde. I will destroy it. I promise."

The eyes flare for an instant then grow dull. The face yellows, the cheeks sink into the skull. There is no repose. Only rage. Death has made her unrecognisable. A macabre, angry, paper puppet.

* * *

He remembers nothing of the drive home. He sees only the mask of pain that was Mathilde. He opens the door and sinks to the floor of his hall, to the cold, hard tiles. He takes the journal from its envelope. Alligator skin, black, luminescent, even after all these years. The clip is missing. Heavy silken paper, gold edging. The writing is formal German script, difficult for him to read, but not impossible. He reads. His face pales, his hands tremble, he is speechless. He sits there, slumped in his anguish. It takes hours for the pain to resolve into rage. A rage so terrible that he thinks his head will burst. And with that rage comes a sort of understanding, a sort of perspective. Eventually he sleeps.

* * *

The phone is ringing again. He gets up from the hall floor, attempts to stretch his cramped body and answers. It is Matron. There will be an autopsy. The funeral will be in three days time at four pm at the Bushey cemetery. He should be at Cameron House by two to accompany her and some of Mathilde's friends.

London, 18th September 1965

What he will say at the funeral? How will he honour this remarkable woman? Her fire, her strength, her wasted life. He will tell the whole story – the sacrifice she made to save him, the lout delivering potatoes, everything. How his very existence was a testimony to her courage. How, by sheer force of will, she had kept his mother alive. How she had survived the worst excesses of the camps, of the slavery, of the Death March. He takes a pen and paper. He will write it down so that nothing is forgotten, so that she is fully honoured for what she has done, what she has been through. But what did he really know of her half-life in the camps, of what she had been forced to do in order to survive? Why had he not asked her? He had been so selfish, so self-absorbed. At least now he would make it up to her.

Delphine is out when he phones. Damn, he had forgotten that they were an hour ahead in France. The hotel receptionist does not know when she will be back. He leaves a stilted message for her to call as soon as she comes in.

"Tell her it is her son, and that it is urgent, you understand. It is about Mathilde. Tell her that Mathilde is dead. Dead. *Mathilde est morte.* She must come to England for the funeral. *Pour l'enterrement,* Tell her I will send a telegram with the details."

CHAPTER 11
London, 20th September 1965

The ungainly limousine falters towards the cemetery, jaded and frayed like some aged gigolo. The black leather upholstery, scarred and worn to shades of grey. The stench of air-freshener and polish overpowering. Michael sits next to Matron, her face ashen, diminished by grief. If only Delphine were here. If only he had heard from her. Where is she?

Two of Mathilde's closest friends face him, casting occasional glances at him and muttering guiltily in Yiddish. Is there venom in their moist eyes? Do they think that he was responsible for Mathilde's final agonies?

The car crawls out of the incongruous, leafy suburbs. Houses become more affluent. Roads wider. Unused fields replace the mansions. Shades of green shine livid in the afternoon sun.

The limousine turns into a narrow country lane and stops. A tractor is blocking its path. An altercation. The youth driving the tractor will not reverse, even though there is a farm track a few yards behind him. Potato lout in another incarnation. Michael can just make out what he is saying.

"Fucking Jews! What a stupid fucking place for a cemetery!"

Michael is stunned, pinioned by his past. Even in death Mathilde is not immune from this poison.

Matron gets out of the car and stands in front of the tractor. A diminutive figure, implacable in hospital blue, complete with upside-down watch and white cap. Arms waving.

"You are going to have to run me over if you want to get down this road, young man. Now move back into that gap! Do it now!"

The youth reddens. He senses the intensity of her feelings. He reverses into the field behind him. The whole process takes less than 30 seconds. Matron returns to the car, primly smoothes her uniform. They drive on.

A few minutes later, the limousine lumbers through black metal gates between high stone walls into an institutional car park. Michael waits while the three woman get out of the car, then follows them. The building is strange, symmetrical, small, rectangular, characterless. A large door open at each end.

Michael is led quickly into the building. Stone floors, chill even on this warm day, as if death never left this place. A primitive two-wheeled cart with rough wooden handles dominates the centre of the room. The white shroud is far too large for Mathilde's tiny coffin. A child's coffin, a broken body. The place is full of people he does not know, the murmuring stops as he enters. The rabbi approaches him. Small, chubby. Billy Bunter with long white beard. His smile is broad, cherubic, inappropriate. One tooth has recently been broken. He does not extend his hand.

"Dr. Turner, I am the Cameron House rabbi. My name is Eric Collins. I will be officiating today. A sad day. After all Mathilde had suffered. She wouldn't see me you know, not once, not even at the end. And yet she wanted a Jewish burial. Such a fighter. Such a fighter."

London, 20th September 1965

His voice is thin, reedy. The words clipped. Faux Oxbridge. He straightens up. He is taller than Michael had thought.

"Right, let's do it. First we must complete the *Keriah,* the ritual rending of your garment."

A few prayers. A knife appears. The rabbi slices right through the lapel of his best suit. Why had he forgotten that this would happen?

They stand, the rabbi gently draws Michael to the front of the group and moves to a small dias. The prayers begin. Words which have meaning for him but no significance. Despite himself he finds he is joining in, swaying, incanting, reciting the *Kaddish.* Lavishing Praise on a God he despises. The prayers end. The bier is being trundled towards the door. Towards the cemetery. Michael catches the rabbi's arm. His movement is too abrupt. The rabbi turns, shocked. The bearers stop.

"Rabbi, please. A few words before we go. I must say something to honour the woman who saved my life. She deserves this at least. Some form of recognition. She must be honoured."

The rabbi's face is stone.

"It is the *Halacha*, the Law. New Moon, There are to be no eulogies on *Rosh Chodesh.* Not here. Not later at the *Shiva.* You cannot speak. I cannot speak. God knows exactly what she has done. That is the only important factor."

He signals to the bearers to continue, and guides Michael firmly forward.

"We cannot insult the Almighty, not at this time. We must save your aunt's soul, at all costs."

The graveside. Tiny pine coffin on rough wooden planks supported by stout ropes. Four huge shovels stand embedded in solid mound of viscous clay. More prayers. Again the *Kaddish.* This time he finds he is crying. The coffin is lowered too fast. It bumps on the floor of the grave, almost tips over. Settles, diminutive in the adult grave. A pause. Some whispering. Michael remembers what he has to do. He steps forward, struggles to dislodge a shovel. The clay is implacable. Immovable. He is crying openly now. Is it frustration, embarrassment or grief? The shovel grows heavier. The clay harder. His attempts weaker. He is perspiring in his ruined suit. He cannot bury her. He cannot bury his past.

A bearded assistant steps forward, takes another shovel and breaks the clods of earth so that Michael can dislodge them. Muffled gunshots as the lumps spatter the box below. Is the coffin empty?

A man puts his hand on Michael's arm. Michael hands him the shovel. The man refuses it and signals that it must be put back in the earth before he can use it. The shovel is replaced in the mud. Earth is scraped into the hole. Other men come forward. Then the grave-diggers take over. Thunderous mounds of clay heap effortlessly. The grave fills.

It is over. They are walking back. Michael finds bearded Billy Bunter by his side. His avuncular smile refashioned into sympathy mode.

"Believe me Dr. Turner...Michael, I can sense how frustrating this must be for you. You took so much effort, spent so much time working out what you would say. How you would honour your aunt. But it was not to be. Perhaps you needed this extra frustration to get in touch with your feelings? Only God knows."

London, 20th September 1965

Grief gives way to rage. How dare this hypocrite hijack such a powerful moment. Michael walks faster, head bowed, silent. The rabbi increases his pace, panting slightly.

"You recited the *Kaddish* very fluently, you have been well taught. But I have a sense that...that you did not 'feel' anything. Perhaps you did not mean what you were saying to the Almighty?"

Despite himself, Michael cannot repress a grim smile. The Almighty? My God? The vengeful God of the Hebrews. The God they worship and revere despite centuries of torture, endless massacres. A continuum of destruction and pain. 'In every generation, they rise up against us.'

They walk in silence between anonymous white marble slabs, vestigies of souls.

"You know Michael, for centuries the Holy Texts were at the centre of our lives. When we emerged from the ghettoes, a gap opened up. A gap between those texts and our core existence. Between the mythical world which had sustained us for so long and the new realities. For so many, Judaism became an encumbrance, a side-show. As it is for you, I fear."

Despite himself Michael finds himself engaging with this sophistry,

"Disconnected from our mythical world, we are inwardly divided. Is that it Rabbi?"

The rabbi grins. He has his dialogue after all. He was beginning to lose hope.

"Ah, I see you know your Jung. Bravo, Dr. Turner, Bravo."

The stones become larger, the graves wider. Names...famous names appear. The occasional mausoleum. Michael's anger takes over again.

"Look Rabbi Collins. It's no use. You can turn this into an intellectual debate. You may even win the argument. But you will not change me. Never. Never."

"Tell me this then Michael, what exactly does your Judaism mean to you?"

Silence. Michael struggles to focus on the question. His shoulders hunch.

"Oh Michael, Michael. I have met so many like you. So many young men like you. Your Judaism is not a living, breathing thing. Not a source of spiritual sustenance. It is dead. It is a series of memories, memories of meaningless rituals, of anti-semitism, each one more painful than the next. Am I wrong?"

Michael remembers the hospital ward when he had scarlet fever – all the other boys calling out 'Jew boy! Jew boy!' while the nurses did nothing. The medical school debating society when they sang "Balls to Mr Banglestein." during his maiden speech. The two men who jumped out of their Porsche shouting "Juden Raus" and gave the Hitler salute. The endless plays and films in which Jews were the slimy villains, the money-grubbing, penny-pinching, devious usurers, the passive victims. Even his new English name, Faigenblum, was against him. After the class read Oliver Twist, he became Fagin until he left that school.

That was the least of it, the easy part. The real pain came from somewhere else. He believed it. Believed it all. Jews did fixate

London, 20th September 1965

about money. They did despise the gentiles. He saw it in his new family. This was no lie. It was true. He saw it in the way his new parents valued possessions above happiness; even saw him as a possession. Hoarded things, enslaved themselves to their God, were unable to smile unless someone told a Jewish joke which belittled them even more. And this was not some hysterical self abasement. This was fact. He had seen the alternative. He had lived it. This was visceral. In his heart he knew that he was not one of these so-called 'Chosen People'. He had had his real life snatched away from him. A life of lightness and joy with Delphine. In favour of what? Some illusory badge of shame?

The Rabbi has put his arm around his shoulder.

"You know Michael, when my son was circumcised, my father had the honour of holding the baby. He could not contain himself. He cried piteously during the whole ceremony. I asked him why he could not be happy for me. I will always remember his words. 'It's not such a good thing to be a Jew in this world.' He was like you, Michael, enmeshed in the past, mired in his own pain. In his own sense of self-pity. But for you. For you there is time. Time to be free. If you can face your anger, anger at yourself, at your heritage. Anger which you have turned into self-hatred."

"So Rabbi, what would you have me do?"

"The answer is so obvious, Michael. It is in your genes. It is there right in front of you. You must find it in yourself, in your actions. That, I cannot help you with."

They stop before a memorial stone. Michael's blood freezes as he reads the words.

> IN EVERLASTING MEMORY
> OF THE MARTYRDOM OF THE HOLY COMMUNITIES
> AND OF THE
> SIX MILLION JEWS
> CRUELLY SLAUGHTERED
> FOR THE
> SANCTIFICATION OF THE
> NAME
> DURING THE HOLOCAUST
> 1939-1945

The rabbi is watching Michael carefully. He knows. He has seen this reaction before, dealt with it before.

"Yes Michael, the terror, the starvation, the torture, the slaughter of innocents, the gas, the death of your sister, your mother, your father, your grandparents, Mathilde. All this was done for the sanctification of God's name. Even those who did not know they were Jews, even those who cursed the Almighty as they went into the gas chamber, even those who did not fight back because they believed that their death was part of a divine purpose. All of it. All of it."

Michael feels as if he has been struck in the face.

"How can that be, rabbi? How?"

"Perhaps after all there is another way of looking at the Holocaust. Even the Talmud allows a Jew to hide his identity if the alternative is death. Let me presume to understand what is in your mind. That perhaps the destruction of all those innocents did not sanctify God's name. Perhaps they changed the way we need

London, 20th September 1965

to look at God. Showed the world the real face of God. At the very least, they made us realise that God was...is, unable to prevent evil. That there are limits to his power."

At last, someone who understands what Michael has been saying for so long.

"Rabbi, you are the first person to have read my mind. That is exactly my view. That is the only way to keep Judaism alive."

The Rabbi's voice is softer, sweeter.

"That is the only way to make sure, completely sure, that Judaism dies, Michael. That Judaism is consigned to oblivion. That is the way to self-destruction. That is tantamount to the acts you revile, to the passive acceptance of our fate. Can you not see that, although God is omnipotent, He has imposed limits on His own power. He has given man free-will. It is not the Almighty you should blame for what happened. This was man's doing. The evil was within man...man...man."

The asthma takes over now. The heaving chest. The tightness. The need for air. Michael fights his body. Forces adrenalin to take over.

"No. No. It cannot be. It cannot be, rabbi. We must re-invent our God. That is the answer to the greatest problem we have ever had to solve."

"And who among us is going to play at being the Almighty, Michael? Who will to have the *hubris* to reformulate our notion of God? A view that we have sustained, that has sustained us, for five thousand years. A view that we have clung to through countless massacres and expulsions and pogroms and persecutions. In all other persecutions the Jews could choose to convert. In this they

Toxic Distortions

had no choice. The demonic nature of the Shoah was precisely that it sought to rob death of this one dignity. Just as the Nazis robbed the victims of their wealth and life, they also robbed them of their humanity."

He takes Michael's arm, and walks him gently towards the exit, the ritual hand washing. The cleansing of the spirit and the body.

"That view of a dichotomy of Deities is exactly what Hitler wanted the world to believe, Michael. That view destroys us as a people for ever. To accept that is to accept that Judaism died in the Holocaust with those who perished. Do you want to give Hitler and his monsters that final victory? Surely you can see the logic of my argument? You must see that."

"I do not see that, rabbi. I see only self-interest. I see a cabal which is too fearful to face the truth, too terrified to save our religion, our race, our identity. It is our only chance. Our only chance. If we fail to accept that our original concept of God's power has changed; that history cannot be ignored, then we will surely lose everything... everything!"

The rabbi's voice, even softer now. He is shaking Michael's shoulder,

"Oh Michael, I urge you to reconsider. Today you are not yourself. You are grieving for the aunt who saved you. Did Mathilde die in vain? Did she die so that you could destroy your heritage? Think about what I have said, please, I beg you."

Michael shakes himself free and walks towards the exit. His face black. He is incandescent. Two women stand there waiting for him. At first he does not focus. He grows closer. Then he sees who they are.

London, 20th September 1965

Delphine has arrived at last. She is standing there with Matron. She moves towards him. Her arms outstretched. She takes his hands, his soaking hands. She looks at his face, his eyes, and sees only blame, blame for what she has done, blame for sending the journal, blame for the death of Mathilde. Her hands slide from his. She crumples into a torrent of sobs, runs to her taxi. The taxi drives off.

He calls after her,

"*Maman, Maman!*"

He has been snatched from his mother's grasp a third time.

PART 2

CHAPTER 1
Munich, 9th November 1965

Franz's clinic is full when the call comes. Sobbing mothers, grim-faced fathers, babies whimpering or silenced by their pain. His whole team is there, registrar, research assistants, students, all eight of them hanging on his every word. So committed. So young.

The caller is brief, cryptic.

"Arte TV now, news bulletin, then call for instructions. Hurry!"

He makes the usual excuse.

"An emergency. Take over please Dr. Schmitz."

Private office locked. Blinds down blanking interior and exterior view. Television image blinking into coherence. Familiar female announcer.

"...and the *GeheimPolitzei* have no doubt that this car bomb was yet another example of Red Army Faction terrorism. Although they have not yet claimed responsibility, it has all the marks of a typical Red Army Faction car bomb attack. And now, an equally disturbing development."

Music. Close-up of squat brick chimney spewing black smoke. Slow pan to crematorium.

At first he thinks it is yet another Holocaust documentary, some sort of colour re-enactment. Cultured female voice. An irritated quality.

"No, not one of the disturbing Auschwitz crematoria images we have seen so often. But there is a connection. A grotesque connection. This sinister picture brings to an end, the life of Dr.Franz Sterberbett. The quiet, peaceful end of Dr.Death as he was known, two days before November the tenth, nineteen sixty-five, the twenty-seventh anniversary of Kristallnacht, pours shame on us all. Not because of the horrific experiments he performed in the camps, but because he lived a free man, because he was allowed to flourish in the very country he had defiled, because he died unpunished, unrepentant. Questions are now being asked – why was he never arrested? Why were telephone taps on his line refused by the authorities?"

A series of stills, surreal images. Pictures he had not seen for years. A younger man in uniform, stern and arrogant. The piercing eyes, the cleft chin. He couldn't help noticing how handsome he had been then. And that scar of his, unmistakeable. They even had one of him getting into a car a year ago in Caracas.

The edgy voice drives on.

"The death of so-called Doctor Sterberbett, who never actually passed his final medical examinations, is a testimony to the duplicity of a nation which professes to atone for the sins of the past, a nation which promised to seek out and punish all those responsible for such obscenities. A will found with his badly mutilated body tells it all. His medical activities in Germany after the war, his business ventures. And all this under the nose of the authorities."

His hand instinctively reaches for the switch. No, he must watch it. He must know what they knew. He must look for clues.

A man appears. A tanned man, of about 60. Straight-backed, powerful shoulders. A confident man. A man he recognises. The

Munich, 9th November 1965

text read 'Chaim Sverovsky'. Of course, he was at Dachau. How did he survive? The voice is grey with bitterness. Perfect German.

"This monster had no pity. His experiments included castration and the removal of other organs without anaesthetic. Injecting gasoline into victims' hearts and watching them die in slow agony. Infecting victims with Dysentery, Typhus and Cholera. He also administered other toxins and recorded the results for pharmaceutical companies. Those of his victims who survived have never been able to find out the name of those drugs, never received compensation. Many of them died in agony simply because our doctors could not find out what had been done to them."

Franz cries out, unaware that he is shouting at the screen.

"I was only there for six weeks, that's all. Six weeks".

More photographs appear. Faces distorted in pain even after death. Medical records with his signature. Even one of himself presenting a paper at a Medical Conference.

A second witness, young Israeli woman.

"There may also be some evidence that Dr Sterberbett's speciality was rubbing broken glass and faeces into the wounds of children as young as three. None survived. He shot them if they were able to withstand the so-called treatment."

He cries out again.

"No, that's not true. No children. Never any children. The others, that was the others. I was not a monster. No children. Never. That was Mengele."

A new face. An elderly woman, still handsome. He remembers the face. Who was it? Sophie, yes Sophie. That wry smile. The voice still full and husky.

"Franz? Yes I knew him. We all knew him. He was a ladies' man. Such a charmer. Of course, we had no idea. All we knew was that he was rich and that he was a doctor. He helped me once with a medical matter, wouldn't accept a fee. Such a charmer, really quite special."

The screen changes. The station's business editor. Please let that be the end of it.

"Dr. Sterberbett's will contains details of bank accounts and safety deposits throughout the world. Funds have been frozen in Switzerland, Austria, Paraguay, Brazil and Argentina...even here in Berlin. Several bankers and accountants are helping the police with their enquiries. The Mossad has seized bullion, diamonds and paintings in Madrid, London and New York."

The news punches the wind from his stomach. He staggers, almost falls. He knows exactly what to do. Dial number, wait, three rings, then hang up. The ring back is instant,

"We have been waiting."

Not his usual contact. This is a new voice, no deference for his age, his position in the organization.

"A car is outside. You will recognise the driver."

The safe-house is set in its own grounds, a squat bunker of a building in an anonymous suburb. A dank, grey, cube with opaque windows. Distorted, dwarf evergreens provide the only foliage.

'Better for surveillance,' he thinks as he walks up the drive. The heavy front door opens instantly to a staircase which leads down three steep flights into a cavernous room hung with damask and silk. Bocara rugs dispel the chill from the tiled floor. No medieval artefacts, no paintings. Just a huge swastika hanging above three

Munich, 9th November 1965

high Bavarian chairs facing a long table. A single low stool waiting for him. Of course, a courtroom. He should have known.

He recognizes two of his interlocutors, or are they interrogators? A dim, improbable memory of camaraderie and misplaced optimism. Bruno and Walter, both grey-faced and irritable. Bruno now has a pony tail and half glasses. That's right, he has become an academic. Organizing student protests no doubt, railing against the authorities. What hypocrisy! But he seems slower, dimmer, somehow diminished.

Walter appears fitter, faster. His forehead and eyes show evidence of expensive plastic surgery. His beard pointed and trimmed like a Conquistador. And the hair? Surely that was new. Walter had been bald even when they were students in Munich. Now he has, what? A toupe? He looks younger than his years, almost attractive, and very, very angry. His eyes glitter with venom.

The third man is younger, straight-backed, correct, but Franz catches the mood at once. He is in charge.

"Thank you for joining us, Herr Doktor."

It was not until he had spoken that Franz realised who he was. That voice. That arrogant sneer. Brinkeren's son. A piranha like his father. The name wouldn't come. Roberto? Carlos? A man used to wealth and privilege, a man used to getting his own way. He spoke again.

"Has he been searched?"

The guard is well-practised. Franz's wallet, keys and loose change are swiftly placed on the long table.

"Please sit down Doktor Von Abgang, I believe that is your current alias, or do you prefer Sterberbett?"

After the slightest of pauses which could have been taken as disrespect, Franz sits, trying to hold himself erect on that child's stool, shading his eyes from the glare of the single spotlight.

"Get to the point, Brinkeren. I worked with your father over twenty years ago. I do not appreciate being treated like a common criminal. I am in no mood for this anachronistic charade."

"Patience, Herr Doktor, patience. You know perfectly well why you are here. We all watched your cremation today. Such a, shall we say, 'convenient' event. You are now a free man. They will call off their search. You accept that, of course?"

Franz knows exactly where this is heading.

"I accept nothing. Whoever did this was..."

"...Whoever did this was on your side Herr Doktor. On your side. Such a convenient event, and at such a convenient time. How is your new wife?"

"She has nothing to do with this."

"Hmm, we shall see. Let us review the evidence. First, you were spotted in Caracas a year or so ago. That scar, your ultimate vanity perhaps. You have resisted every request to have it removed. As a result you have been forced to evade Wiesenthal, the Mossad, Fortune Hunters. Second, you have a beautiful young wife from a respectable family. Left wingers I believe."

Bruno is looking increasingly uncomfortable. Tapping his fingers with increasing nervousness.

"For God's sake Franz, it's obvious. They were closing in on you. You had to do something.

Brinkeren drives on, barely hesitating.

Munich, 9th November 1965

"You are no longer young. Perhaps you have had enough of being spied on. Perhaps you need time to enjoy your new family. Time to run your clinic without employing an army of minders. Without bribing politicians…police chiefs."

Walter's face suffuses with choler.

"You are the only one of us who never needed the money. Your 'family dynasty…industry, pharmaceuticals, you had millions then. The clinic, the real estate in Berlin, the golf clubs in Spain. Admit it. You betrayed us. You betrayed the organisation."

Bruno is cleaning his glasses furiously. His voice is thin, reedy, no longer strident.

"Please Walter, that's not how we….look Franz, you and I, the old days. Comrades, even friends. At this stage no-one is actually accusing you of…"

He writhes in his chair. The words force themselves from him.

"The difficulty we have is…well apart from the four of us, no-one, no-one at all had all the information. The secret numbers, the bullion. And there it was, in your will. In your will!"

Brinkeren raises his hand, clearly irritated by Bruno's manner.

"As you are no doubt aware, Herr Doktor, almost every one of our organisation's assets have been frozen. By now they will have been seized. Several of our business associates are in custody. Many will talk. After all, their ideology, if you can call it that, is purely venal. They have nothing to lose; everything to gain. Names are being whispered, the rumours reach to the very core of government.

"We must all face the fact that this set-back could spell the end of our organisation. It will certainly mean that dependants of our colleagues will receive nothing in future.

"This tribunal needs to be convinced that you did not come to an arrangement with our enemies. You have ten minutes."

Franz gets to his feet very slowly and pauses for effect. He stands erect, making full use of his height, his presence.

"First gentlemen, let me say that I fully understand your concerns. As you all know, I have played an essential role in the development of our organization, opening channels of communication with key figures in financial institutions, initially in Switzerland and then, further afield. Legitimising our position by oiling the wheels with government officials and religious leaders. Let there be no mistake. This is a carefully constructed plan. There are so many falsehoods about me in this report. We are dealing with ruthless enemies here. Many people with the same hatred, the same vengefulness. It is clear to me, as it will be to you when I have completed my exposition, that this situation has been devised in order to destroy the sense of trust and honour we have always maintained at the highest level.

"I have no idea how this financial information was leaked. We only know that the leakage was comprehensive. And it is clear to me that it was one of us. But whoever did this must have had a motive. Me? I have no motive whatsoever. I have millions – in Saudi Arabia, Egypt, Switzerland. More money than I can ever spend. Huge sums which no-one will find. I could leave for Chile tomorrow, live out my life in obscene luxury and still leave enough for two or three generations. It makes no sense for me to incur your wrath; to put my life at risk. No sense at all. Surely you can see that. But there is another reason why I could not have done this. A far more compelling argument. Those of you who know

Munich, 9th November 1965

me will be aware that I live …that I have always lived…by a strict code of honour, that I am physically incapable of such a despicable act. My honour. My family's honour could never…."

Franz is just about to launch himself into a stirring avowal of his family motto, his loyalty to the organisation, to the memory of the Fuhrer, when an orderly in full motorcycle gear enters unannounced and hands Brinkeren a file which he skims quickly and passes to the others. The shock registers instantly on their faces. Walter has a convulsive coughing fit. No words are exchanged between them. Brinkeren's tone is granite.

"Herr Doktor, we have just received some grave news. This new intelligence comes from the highest authority. It appears that, two hours before all the accounts were frozen, the cumulative sum of five million dollars was withdrawn from our accounts in Germany, Switzerland and Austria. It was then deposited in newly opened accounts in the name of Berthe Gonzales, who I understand to be the daughter of your sister. Five million dollars."

Franz's control slips away. He feels the perspiration accumulating in his armpits, on his upper lip.

"For God's sake, Brinkeren. These people are not stupid. They are sophisticated. They are chess players. They have anticipated my defense. Anyone could have used Berthe's name, faked her identity. Anyone. This is a trick, a naive trick. Punish me and you will lose the trust of all our members, you will…"

Brinkeren stands abruptly. The other two follow. The guard moves closer.

"You will now be taken to an antechamber where you will await our verdict."

Despite all his training, all his conditioning, a terrible rage possesses Franz. None of his pursuers would do what his so-called colleagues intended. None would be so barbaric. He steps forward, his voice vibrating with fury.

"Before this travesty of a court pronounces sentence on me. I wish to make a statement. Those of you who served in the SS knew only too well what happened in those final years. You can no longer lie to yourselves. What you did was worse, far worse than the worst excesses of the most rapacious Jews in history. No Jew in history has killed millions out of greed. No Jew in history murdered and tortured purely in order that he and his family could live in luxury for generations. Whatever your ideology in those early days, whatever illusions you may have had then about making the world *Judenrein*, none of this made any sense after El Alamein, Stalingrad, Chernahy, Bari. By January 44 you all knew the war was lost. You all knew that the Jews of Russia, Switzerland, Albania, Bulgaria, England, Ireland, Palestine, America, Canada, Australia were beyond your reach. You murdered millions simply in order to steal, simply in order to eliminate the witnesses to your crimes.

"While I was aborting foetuses from rape victims on the Eastern front, you Walter, were carrying out Selektions in Dachau, you Bruno were sending thousands of Salonikan Jews to their death. Your father, Brinkeren was blackmailing Hungarian Jews in return for the lives of a few thousand of their people.

"Greed. Greed is why you killed. Greed is why you tortured. You are the Jews! You are the Jews!"

Brinkeren waves his hand imperceptibly, the slightest of movements. Franz is led outside. He does not need to hear the barely audible argument. It does not take long. Three minutes. Three minutes for a man's life.

Brinkeren intones the verdict. Almost priest-like.

"Having examined all the evidence, we find Doctor Franz Sterberbett, alias Doctor Franz Von Abgang, guilty of conspiring with the enemy to reveal the whereabouts of our resources. Guilty of stealing five million dollars, Guilty of betraying the SS. You will be executed by a firing squad of your peers. The sentence will be carried out immediately."

He is taken down another flight of stairs to a sound-proofed room. A sand-bagged post stands against the far wall which is pocked with holes. They had done this before.

The guard leads Franz to the post and secures his arms. He is offered a blindfold which he refuses.

Brinkeren, Bruno and Walter are no more than 2 metres away from him when they take aim. He tries to stare at them, to make them look at him when they pull the trigger, but his eyes fill with tears and he squeezes them shut to hide his shame. Brinkeren gives the order.

"Raise your weapons, aim, fire!"

The sound is amplified tenfold by the enclosed space. Smoke fills the room. When it clears, Franz is kneeling, whimpering silently. He has soiled himself, pale yellow excrement seeps from his trousers. Urine flows around him. The stench is appalling.

Disgust distorts Walter's face.

"He has become a Mussulman. Shit inside. Shit outside."

Brinkeren gives the orders.

"Cut him down and dump him on the steps of his clinic. Tonight when you are not seen. He is not to change before he leaves. Prepare the car carefully."

* * *

The young registrar is clearly shocked. So different. The drawn grey-green, asymmetric face, the contorted mouth, the anxious darting eyes. So different from the Herr Professor, his mentor, his friend – a man of vigour, of supreme confidence. He chooses his words carefully. The woman is distraught enough as it is.

"Frau Von Abgang, your husband has suffered a massive stroke. I will try to test which of his faculties are still active. Do you wish to leave the room?"

The woman shakes her head. Schmitz goes to work at once. A small sound alarm is placed against each ear in turn. On both occasions, the head jerks away as the alarm is pressed. A light is shone in each eye causing instant reactions. A small hammer tests muscular reflexes. There are none. A beaker of water checks the swallowing reflex provoking gagging and choking. A small needle to the finger shows that there is pain as the hand is jerked away.

"It is as I suspected, Frau Von Abgang. He cannot move or speak or swallow, but he can see and hear and feel pain. In these cases it is probable that he can also understand what is being said to him. You must speak to him, give him hope. Tell him he will recover. Keep talking. His eyes may fill with tears. This will be distressing for you, but it is a good sign. A sign that he can understand. We will feed his body, but you, you must feed his

Munich, 9th November 1965

spirit. In doing that you will keep him alive. That is the priority. There is no certainty, but there have been miraculous remissions. Not complete recovery, but miraculous nonetheless. Bring a radio next time you come, or a gramophone, play him his favourite music. That will definitely help. Do not give up hope."

Schmitz backs slowly out of the room as Frau Von Abgang throws herself on the bed and cradles Franz's gargoyle head in her arms murmuring endearments, singing little snatches of a love song. Franz's eyes flood. He has heard what was said, but he already knew the real prognosis.

CHAPTER 2
Munich, 5th November 1965

The following afternoon Franz has a visitor. Walter, impeccable in Saville Row suit, gold tipped walking stick, matching leather briefcase and hand-made shoes. He closes and locks the door, positions himself so that he can be seen by Franz and smiles warmly.

"Ah Franz, poor Franz. Things have worked out better than I expected, much better. What an arrogant fool you are. Such a pious speech. Honour, family honour. Was it honourable to eviscerate pregnant women and torture children? OK, so you did your stealing before we did and you used that money to bribe your way out of trouble, to build successful businesses. You did not murder in order to steal like the rest of us, but you stole and murdered just the same.

"And your 'You are the Jews' speech. Do you think the irony was lost on me? On any of us? Do you think we had no idea how much the SS were stealing for themselves in the camps? Why Eichmann insisted on Argentinian currency in his negotiations with the Hungarian Jews? Was that money the Third Reich would ever see? Brinkeren was going to let you off with a massive fine until you made that speech. 'You are the Jews.' What rubbish.

"Let me tell you something. However many Jews we killed, it was not enough. Not enough. Five years ago I went to Verona to hear the *Aida* there. I took my wife, Frieda, I think you might remember her, even after all these years. Yes, I am sure you would have memories of her."

He pauses, takes out a cigarette, taps it on a cigarette case and lights it slowly.

"We had booked the best seats of course. The same seats I had sat in for five years, the perfect acoustic. We edged our way along the fifth row to our places. Someone was in our place. I was aware of a tall man in a grey open-necked shirt, about seventy, with a pretty, younger woman. Frieda politely pointed out to him that he was in our seats. He felt in his pockets and showed her his tickets. A classic Italian mistake. They had given us adjacent places, not those which I had always sat in. Frieda asked if he would mind changing places since we had sat in those seats for years. He was polite but firm. No, he would not move. He had chosen these seats for the perfect acoustic. So we pushed past him and sat down. He turned and smiled at me. He thought it was a great joke. Then I saw it. The gold Star of David around his neck. Not brash but small and finely wrought. My hands began to tremble. I could feel the blood draining from my face, the rage overtaking me. I tried to get up and leave but Frieda stopped me."

"The Jew grinned broadly and looked straight past me as if I were invisible, spoke only to Frieda. 'What's the matter with your husband?' 'I think you know,' she said, 'Oh yes, *Gnadige Frau*, I know. I know very well.' He was mocking me, mocking me with his strength, his confidence, his very presence. There was no hatred in him, only a vague, awareness of what I might have done.

"As you might expect, I did not enjoy the first act. The Jew seemed to be leaning into me. I could feel the pressure of his arm on mine, his knees splayed outwards forcing me to cross my legs. At the interval he got up and leaned right over me. 'Look after my coat for me, there's a good chap, I'll be back in a few minutes.' It was an order, not a request. I felt frozen, immobile. He came back fifteen minutes later and grinned his thanks. It is something of an understatement to say that I heard nothing that evening.

"That night, as has been my practice since school, I went through my pockets and placed everything on my bedside table. Wallet, passport, money. As I was feeling for my lira, something sharp slid under my finger nail. The pain was intense. When I checked again, I saw what it was. The Jew had slipped his Star of David into my pocket. I should have told Frieda, thrown it away at once, but I didn't. I put it in my glasses case and kept it. I want you to have it."

He pulls back the bed cover and slips the gold star deftly under Franz's toe-nail without drawing blood. Franz's leg quivers. Walter pauses, takes out another cigarette and lights it, watching the rage in Franz's eyes.

"But that is not why I am here Franz. I am here for a completely different reason. I am here to tell you why I betrayed you. After all, if you are to be paralysed and mute for the rest of your life, you should at least know why."

He takes a velvet cloth from his briefcase and unwraps it to reveal a black alligator skin journal with gold-edged pages. The clasp missing. The year 1943 embossed on the front in filigreed gilt lettering.

"Frieda died last year after a long illness, neurasthenia, depression. Such a painful thing to see someone you have loved and tended for twenty five years torture herself into oblivion. She did get very agitated before her death, tried to speak, she kept saying 'Destroy it. Destroy it.' Then faded instantly."

He opens the journal.

"I recently came into possession of her journal. A well-wisher recently sent it to me at the Hospital in Dortmund, said it had been left at the nursing home after her death. I thought you might be intrigued to hear what she said about you. It is from the time when we were stationed at Dachau together."

Walter reads as if reciting a shopping list.

"'March 3rd - Something strange happened today and I am confused by it, rather shocked really. Strange that I should have decided to start my journal today. Perhaps I had a feeling that something momentous would happen, who knows? Franz and I were in the library. So few books and most of them propaganda. He leaned over me to see what I was reading and passed his hand lightly, oh so lightly over my bottom. The sensation was unlike anything I had experienced, an exquisite touch. Over in seconds as I moved quickly away.

March 4th - I found myself back in the library again looking out for Franz. I waited an hour and just as I was about to leave, he came in. He gave no sign that he was looking for me. We wandered aimlessly about the library for a few minutes. To my surprise I found that I was manoeuvring my body so that I would be leaning over a book with my back to him. He took no notice at first. Then that touch again, gossamer to start with, but his hand felt through my legs and into my vagina. I was already open, moist. I began to groan and sway. He whispered 'Sorry' and left.

March 5th - Last night I made love to Walter more passionately than I had for years. He was quite surprised, but it was clear that he enjoyed every minute. Maybe that is just what we needed to rekindle the lust of our early years? I sincerely hope so. Thank you Franz.

March 6th - What have I done? What on earth have I done? Franz rang me today. He wanted to apologise for his behaviour. It was inexcusable. I should have immediately accepted his apology and hung up. Instead when he said 'Goodbye' I whispered, 'Don't go', in a small husky voice, a voice I didn't even recognise. He got the inference at once. He was a sophisticated man. 'Be careful of Franz, he is dangerous', they all said that, all the women.

The old lines are the best. Was I interested in photography? Would I like to see his images of rare birds. Rhetorical question! I see him tomorrow. Something tells me Walter will enjoy tonight!'"

Walter breaks off and wipes his eyes.

"Frieda – my Frieda. She was so scientific in her descriptions, her nursing background no doubt."

A thought darkens his brow.

"Perhaps she read these pages for years afterwards? Perhaps she was thinking of you every time we made love. Who knows?"

His hands tremble violently as he turns the pages.

"'*March 7th - A completely novel experience. So slow, so considerate. First that stroking hand – no kissing. None at all at that stage. Then he undressed me sliding the back of his fingers over my nipples again and again, faster and faster until they were almost bursting. And when I was on the point of orgasm, he lifted me onto the bed and spread my legs wide apart. His penis was less than a millimetre from me, I could feel its heat, but he would not touch me. I strained forward but he pulled back laughing. 'You must learn to be patient,' he said. Then, he pushed in and out of the entrance. In and out as the lips swelled and gorged with blood. I felt I was dying with pleasure. He pulled away from me and started kissing my lips for the first time, just the corners of my mouth. I opened my mouth and his tongue moved with mine. That's when I realised that he had entered me again. Fully, deeply, stroking so slowly it was difficult to realise he was moving. I had never tried such a slow movement before – the only word I can think of is 'exquisite', exquisite pleasure. Orgasm after orgasm. I was literally out of my mind by this time. And just when I thought that there could be no feeling more intense, nothing more unbelievably arousing, he started to stroke in and out faster, more forcefully. Removing his penis at every stroke and inserting it again to its hilt while at the same time delicately manipulating my clitoris with his fingers. My body was churning. My mind was bursting with pleasure. Then he came in me. He came for hours, groaning and spurting until his weight settled down into me. Even then he was still big. He grinned and reached for two cigarettes. I didn't smoke but I took it and pretended to puff away.*

March 10th - The past few days have merged into a strange sensual dream, intense, all-consuming. We have made love so many times. I am amazed that Walter has noticed nothing. It is true that he has enjoyed better sex than ever for the past three nights. He must have been amazed by my passion. So easy. All I had to do is imagine Franz's fingers probing me, his penis at the entrance to my clitoris and I am already orgasming.

March 11th - Franz has gone. Left without a word. He must have known, must have received his postings weeks ago. So I was a little diversion, a plaything, someone to be corrupted, despoiled and put aside like an old toy. I will never forgive him. Never.

March 25th - I have tried everywhere. No-one can tell me where he was posted. My body is turning in on itself. I masturbate the whole time

Munich, 5th November 1965

thinking of the way he touched me and stroked inside me. I am destroyed. Utterly bereft.

April 5th - This cannot be. It cannot be. I have checked and re-checked my calendar a hundred times. It cannot be. My time. I have missed my time. After all these years. A son. A son for Walter. The son he has always craved. He will be so happy. A baby boy of our own, to love and hold and educate. An honourable man like Walter. At last something to dull the pain of Franz…. Franz? No. No, it can't be Franz's baby. It must not be Franz's baby. Wait. It is so simple. I will make love to Walter tonight, passionate love, and again tomorrow night. I will make it so memorable for him. Something he will never forget. If the baby is a few weeks early, he will not even notice. He will be too delighted to have a son to even think about it.

April 6th - Sweet Jesus help me. Help me decide what to do. I keep seeing <u>his</u> face, his long face. Those piercing blue eyes, that cleft chin. It is his creature which is growing inside me. Sucking my life's blood. I know it is. His creature. A child of lust. A child of sin. A child of evil. I cannot do it. I cannot bring the offspring of something so vile into this world. I cannot. I know what I must do. I will go to Berlin tomorrow. God forgive me.'"

Walter closes the diary, wraps it carefully in the velvet cloth, and puts it back in his briefcase.

"You know Franz, I had always thought that her sudden depression was my fault, that she had somehow heard about my freezing experiments on the young Polish officers. Now I realise that her breakdown was the result of a different crime."

He puffs slowly on his cigar for some time.

"So now you know why you are here. Why you are dying in this ignominious, this humiliating way with your bedpans and bottles. Unable to touch your manhood. Able only to see, to hear... and to feel."

Walters turns towards the door.

"Oh, by the way, in case you are wondering, it was me who suggested blanks. The others wanted a more, shall we say, 'final' solution."

He looks at Franz for a long time.

"Let me see. What do I wish you? I know. Yes, it's perfect. I wish you what Jews wish one another after a funeral. 'I wish you a long life', a very long life."

He strides from the room.

* * *

Walter had never thought for one moment that he would be grateful for the Red Army Faction. Despicable worms who wanted to destroy everything he had ever believed in. But they saved his life. Without their car-bomb campaign he would have been vaporised.

As he reaches the hospital car park he can see that some uniformed police have gathered around his Porsche. They are still checking the underside with a mirror as he approaches the cordon.

"Something wrong officer?" he asks the young sergeant.

"This your car sir?"

"No, just curious."

Munich, 5th November 1965

"I must ask you to move away, we've already found one bomb. There may be more."

So Brinkeren had bugged Franz's hospital room. They must have suspected him from the start. Walter ducks back into the hospital and emerges ten minutes later from a side entrance. He is wearing a white lab coat and has a stethoscope around his neck. He is bald, completely bald. And his beard has gone.

He must leave at once. Before they try again. He uses the U-bahn. Taxis were dangerous, they could be traced. At Frankfurt station he takes the first train out of Germany.

CHAPTER 3
Geneva, 28th November 1965

"No use pretending my friend, I see it in your face, you too have known suffering, but yours is from a long time ago. Mine is...mine is..."

The man is tall, angular. His once handsome face dusted with white stubble, his breath reeks of stale whisky.

"Mine is too..."

He is gripping Michael's shoulders gazing fiercely into his eyes. He starts to cry.

The place was hard to find in the dusk. A narrow doorway sandwiched between a dry cleaners and a working man's cafe off a nondescript Geneva street in the commercial district. Stairs leading down to a peeling grey door embellished with an amateurish picture of a machine gun and a sign 'The Mercenary.' A door which opens to the sound of a piercing air raid siren alarm and a confusion of war.

Along one wall, glass cases full of swords, scimitars, rapiers, bejewelled Moroccan daggers, pikes and bludgeons. In front of him a small stage, a Tussauds of blond models in every rank of German uniform. Panzer and Luftwaffe officers, Afrika Corps tank commanders with helmet and goggles, SS Scharfuhrers with daggers. Some wore huge, leather great-coats, others shorts and desert boots. Then, a surreal touch, the same blond, young mannequin wearing full Chelsea Pensioner's regalia complete with medals and walking stick. Behind the stage another display, red silk scarves and arm bands, cufflinks, ceremonial daggers, eagles, buckles, belts, boots. And everywhere the swastikas, iron crosses, SS flashes and death's heads. A low table crammed with re-enactments of the great tank battles of Kursk and Tobruk, model planes, Heinkels and Stukas hang from ceiling wires. Another table is loaded with medals, ceremonial knives and daggers. The face of Hitler, the identical iconic image, peers eerily at Michael from countless frames, some old, some new and gleaming. On the farthest wall, a collage of Reifenstahl photographs – idyllic Aryan children skipping hand in hand, perfect black bodies, implausible athletes, silhouettes of helmeted robots, Nuremberg arms in serrated homage.

The man's voice, distraught.

"What is it called in your country? Yes, of course you use the same word, a *cliché*. The younger man and the rich woman. Do you know what she did this morning? Told the authorities that I had no residence permit! I, Vittorio Bruneschini who have lived in this boring, safe country for nearly fifteen years!"

He struggles with his over-tight jeans and pulls out a crumpled photograph of a smiling, confident couple, easy with one another, standing next to a large white sports car. She, small, slightly overweight with huge breasts, excessive make-up, high-heeled, an arm extended so that her hand can stroke the nape of the man's strong neck. His arm draped over her shoulder. And yes, Michael can see. In another world, another time, the ravaged face would have been recognisable.

"Here, here's a picture taken only three months ago. Would you even know it was me?"

Geneva, 28th November 1965

He looks up in supplication.

"Oh Theresa, Theresa. Did I tell you that she's taken everything. The villa in Positano, the cars, the horse, the boat, the nightclub, everything. Except this shop, where I started out. That, at least, she left me, but only so that I can pay her alimony."

He grabs a pink silk puppet then a clone of the first in pale blue. Twines them together in an erotic mingling, a splaying of legs, a lifting of buttocks.

"You see these two Harlequins. Real silk that is. Diamonds for eyes. I had them made on our fifth wedding anniversary. That's how in love we were then. Couldn't get enough of one another. Now it makes me sick to look at them."

Then he is himself again. A merchant, a salesman.

"So what brings you here to my little shop, monsieur?"

Michael has rehearsed the answer.

"I am having a party. A fancy dress party."

The man is almost smiling now, he grimaces his anguish away.

"A 'themed' fancy dress party, monsieur?"

"Exactly."

"I understand. I understand perfectly. You have come to the right place."

He clicks his fingers and a bent stick-woman of indeterminate age and colour appears.

"Two coffees. Ristretto. Now."

The woman disappears and instantly brings two tiny cups.

Michael sips the mud trying not to grimace his disgust at the taste. The man starts to weep again. Michael gambles.

"Look, you are clearly not in the mood to..."

Vittorio grabs his arm.

"No, please don't leave, I must tell someone. I can't just stay here on my own. Please, I will give you a big discount for your party."

Michael disengages himself.

"OK, I'll stay for a bit."

Vittorio's eyes show his relief.

"Thank you. I will not keep you long. I promise."

He looks aimlessly around the shop. Then the words pour out. A torrent of pain.

"Oh you will not believe my friend, how things were at the beginning...when we first met. I was an athlete, a model. I had to lock my hotel room at night just to get some sleep! Wait a minute, I've got them here somewhere."

He scrabbles with a photographic album on a small table and muses over it.

"Ah yes here they are. I know that one's a bit creased, but you can still see what I looked like. That's me modelling haircream. Here look at these...I've got lots of cuttings. Ah here's another one. Now what was that? Oh yes Maserati. Can you imagine, me? Maserati cars? I had my whole life ahead of me. I was a God, fearless, ready to seize every opportunity...the little kid from the slums of Napoli was going to make it big. Look at me now. Some joke eh?"

Michael changes the subject.

"Where did you meet?"

Vittorio smiles dimly.

"At Cuneo's...you don't know it? Oh it's one of the most famous restaurants in Hamburg, Italian food. Just next to the Reeperbahn,

Geneva, 28th November 1965

where these women sit in rows like butcher's meat and fake an orgasm as you walk past their huge department store windows. It was near the photographic studios where I was modelling at the time. Some of us used to take time out and go and fuck an enormous whore in the middle of the day.

"Have I shocked you? Well, perhaps if you remember that I'm the son of a prostitute who sold herself to every soldier and sailor in Naples during the war, Moroccan, German, Brits, Yanks, black, white and brown, you won't expect so much of me.

"I was there on my own, eating Tagliatelli, going through my lines for a film. Oh yes, I was in films too, and she came in with a group of people. The place was packed, but you know those German restaurants - they squeeze you in even when there's no room - on those long trestle tables where everyone sits together. And she arranged things so that she'd be sitting next to me. No, it's true. She told me afterwards...later that night in fact.

"Typical spoilt rich kids I thought. And then I felt this hand sliding up inside my thigh. She was talking and joking with her friends, looking away from me, and stroking me at the same time. I couldn't believe it at first. What do you when that happens? Call for the manager? Of course I was flattered. No-one had ever done that before, oh yes, lots of women had asked me, but nothing like that, not in public.

"Couldn't even turn to look. I nearly choked on my pasta when it started. Then I just opened my legs and turned a bit towards her so that she could get a good grip, you know. A bit later, I went to the gents to finish things off, and she was standing there waiting for me when I came out. We left without paying the bill."

He looks at Michael's face. Some movement of his forehead, has made Vittorio aware.

"Oh please, you don't think I'd have gone for some ugly bitch just because she wanked me off in a restaurant do you? No, she was beautiful, she turned heads. Big tits, long red hair, freckles, God I loved those freckles, sexy as hell, and aching for me, aching for me all the time. That's all there was at first, the screwing, night and day. We couldn't keep our hands off one another. I remember one cocktail party her father gave when we did it in his immaculate bedroom. The trouble is, she was a screamer. You should have seen her father's face when we came back downstairs.

"But her father hated me even before that night. He'd had me checked out by his friends, real friends, I mean. There was a file on me of course, there was one on all of us. He knew exactly who I was, what I was. But I knew him too. Oh yes we all knew him in those days. Five years, they gave him, five years in some comfortable prison. He served three, then took a train straight to Switzerland. They all did as soon as they could raise the cash, and that wasn't difficult. There was always someone ready to help, at a price. Then the usual stuff, a change of name, a new identity, a business to buy."

A cue.

"So that's how you started *The Mercenary?*"

"Of course. By the time I met Theresa her dad was already very rich. Not surprising when you start your post war career with a few million in diamonds and old masters. I think he would have had me eliminated, what did they use to call it? "Special treatment". But he didn't dare. If she'd suspected anything, anything at all....

Geneva, 28th November 1965

well, that would have been the end of his life. To be rejected by his daughter, his only child, as well as the wife he'd lost when she was born."

Vittorio sips his coffee and lights a cigarette. This is better. He feels calmer.

Michael presses on.

"And where did you marry?"

Vittorio smiles and goes back to the photograph album.

"In Hamburg, big society wedding. Look, here's the headline "Aphrodite and her Adonis." See that, even then while they were taking the picture, she couldn't keep her hands off me. How tall, how straight I was then! Did I tell you I haven't slept for ten days. I lie down in our beautiful flat, on the bare floorboards. She didn't even leave me a sleeping bag, generous eh? And pictures keep coming, pictures of us together. Last night as soon as I closed my eyes I thought I was in our soft bed with the silk sheets, with all our beautiful things. Paintings, sculptures around me, and she was lying next to me stroking me, whispering 'Liebchen, liebchen,' like she used to...and I was crying and she was saying, 'I'm back, I'm back. The nightmare is over.'"

Michael watches him very closely. There is a lot more that Vittorio needs to say.

"How long did you live in Germany?"

"We didn't stay there. Came straight here after the wedding. Her father wanted me in another country. I suppose he didn't trust me to keep my mouth shut. Well of course he gave me money, a lot of money. His daughter was used to the best. You think he wanted her to have to dirty her fingers or bargain for food in the markets?

"And you were successful?"

"If you have money my friend, it's easy to make more. First this shop. Ok her father started me off, but I knew exactly where to get all these things, what do they call it now? Military memorabilia. Old friends in Italy. They were keeping them, and they needed cash. That was easy. What do you say in your country? 'Money talks?' It did in those days my friend, money got you whatever you wanted. Then I started travelling, buying, Went to Austria, France, England. Moved into other areas, stamps, old currency."

"So you were a real success."

Vittorio stands, takes a wad of hundred dollar bills out of his pocket and starts throwing them on the floor one by one.

"This is how rich I was. Cash businesses, always the best. Nightclubs. No-one really knows how much you take. And if there's a bit of gambling or sex going on, so what?

"Life was good, really good. Did I tell you she liked to sing? Theresa. That's why I bought the first club. She was great, on the radio a lot, made a few records, romantic stuff. Nothing too sexy. I wouldn't let her. I hated it when men leered at her. Nearly killed some kid for trying to put money down the top of her dress. You see it never stopped, the sex. She'd come into my office and lock the door. She'd come so quickly, again and again. It got easier and easier. And we had that, what would you call it? That tradition. Yes, sex in public places. I'd make her come in restaurants, in the cinema. She loved that. We both did. She always kept a spare pair of panties in her bag. She used to joke about cleaners finding those expensive panties in toilets all over Geneva and not knowing whether to hand them in or take them home. She'd make up little jokes about what they told their husbands?"

Michael waits for his moment.

"And then something happened."

Vittorio's face goes grey.

"Yes, something happened. Overnight. It wasn't enough for her, for Theresa. She had everything, everything. First she got into Yoga and meditation. That was too hard. So then she wanted a child, a baby of her own. But she had been having some...problems, you know. So we went to the doctor and they did the tests."

Vittorio falters. Michael pours him some water and helps him drink.

"This is too much for you."

"No, please monsieur, I must go on. I must. I cannot stop now. Please, hear my story. Please."

He waits until Michael inclines his head.

"The doctor said that it would be very dangerous for her to have babies. That we should adopt."

"Did he tell you why?"

Vittorio falters, trying to dredge up some medical name.

"Some disease, woman's disease. We had a terrible fight about it. She was desperate for a child. Said she didn't care if it was dangerous. I couldn't lose her, you see, loved her too much."

Vittorio is breathing faster now. His breath rasping in his chest.

"Then she got pregnant. Stopped using her coil without telling me. I was so angry....I beat her up. For the first time in our... beat her up. She pleaded with me to let her have the baby and I beat her up!"

He is crying again.

"How did she react?"

"Do you know, she forgave me. Said that her father used to do it to her mum all the time. I bought her a big present of course. A racehorse."

"Hoping she'd ride it. Did it work?"

Vittorio's eyes glint. This man is not stupid.

"No. So I had to do something...something else."

Vittorio stops again. Michael talks to him calmly.

"So you did something. What?"

Vittorio chokes out the words.

"I drugged her, took her to a friend. A private clinic. They did it. Said I had saved her life."

"And how did she react?"

Vittorio shrugs.

"Oh she was low of course. But didn't throw things like she did when she found out I'd been to a whore."

"And then?"

"After that I wouldn't fuck her any more. Couldn't trust her. Knew she'd try again. The bitch was *pazza*, Completely crazy. She begged me, used to try to touch me and give me an erection while I was asleep and put me inside her. But I couldn't take the chance. Couldn't lose her."

Michael hands Vittorio the water. He finishes the rest of the glass in one long gulp.

"How did she take it?"

"That's when things really went wrong. First she started losing her temper all the time. Then she spent days in bed crying and sleeping. It was the fucking that had kept us together, you see. That was the only thing we had. There was nothing else."

"So what happened?"

"She was making secret phone calls all the time. Used to put the phone down as soon as I came in. Then she started going out after I'd left for work. The maid told me. One night she came back late and said she'd met this young English psychiatrist who could cure her. Some expert or other. Asked me for a lot of money to go to some clinic in Zurich. Why did I give it to her? Why?"

Michael times his response carefully,

"And did she come back?"

"Oh yes she came back all right. She came back while I was out. Just last week. I got home at six as usual. The house had been stripped. Both cars gone. Not even a note. Got a call in the shop the next day from some Yid lawyer. Something about proceedings. I didn't listen, just shouted 'Fuck off' and put the phone down."

Vittorio starts to weep. Michael stands,

"That is a very sad story *signore*. One of the saddest I have heard. You are clearly very upset by what has happened. I am sure that this is not the best time for us to conduct our business. It must be very near to your closing time anyway. I will come back tomorrow. Tomorrow at ten o'clock."

Michael extends his hand.

Vittorio sees that he is about to lose a customer. Something he has never done in his twenty years as a businessman. His smile reveals expensive dental work but no joy.

"Please sir. Forget this nonsense of mine. It was nonsense. Of no importance. We will do business, yes?"

Michael, withdraws his hand and inclines his head. Vittorio bustles him towards the back of the shop.

"You want costumes for a special party. I have the best. The most authentic in Switzerland, maybe in the world. Originals."

They duck through a small door. Huge oak desk surrounded by dress rails from which uniforms are arranged according to their size. German army uniforms, Waffen SS. Something else. Something which snatches at Michael's throat. Striped jackets and trousers, concentration camp clothes, forlorn, torn, frayed. Originals, ten of each with a different coloured triangle, red, black, yellow, pink.

Vittorio goes to a rail and pulls out a uniform.

"Here, monsieur, this is an *Obersturmbahnfuhrer*. The kind of thing you are looking to wear, or do you want a higher rank?"

He gestures to the striped jackets.

"The girls will be in these garments, yes?"

The front door bell sounds. The same air raid siren.

Vittorio is confused.

"Shit! Forgot to lock up after you came in. Excuse me for one minute. I will get rid of this person. Please look around. Try this one on. It is your size."

He turns and leaves. A few minutes pass. Muffled voices. A commercial exchange. Michael can hear a familiar French voice and smell Gauloise.

He goes to the desk and searches quickly through the drawers. Then he finds it. A small brown book. He flicks through the book and notes down a name and address in southern England. Then he puts the book back exactly where it was and walks out past two men haggling furiously over a Ceremonial sword encrusted with agates in swastika patterns.

CHAPTER 4
Bournemouth, 12th December 1965

Columns, counters, crowds. Bournemouth's main post office, chandeliered, palatial and seedy. Always so busy on Fridays. Frayed pensioners queuing for their meagre cash. Frazzled mothers with prams and cheques from the Labour Exchange. Bored porters with parcels. Businessmen bullies with distinguished watches and dismissive frowns. No-one paid any attention to the tall man, bald and erect, who queued patiently until his time came, produced his passport, and received a small envelope. No-one that is, except a young, blond man in dark glasses, lounging in a corner.

* * *

Light. Light everywhere. Light bursting from the candelabra planted on the grand piano. The menorah of all menorahs, huge, heavy, solid, golden. Light on the acres of latke laden tables. Light fizzing from the sparklers of the young boys, sidelocks and tzizit dancing as they weave their fiery wands into glimmering curves. Light in the eyes of the roaming pre-pubescent girls, covered from head to toe in their velveteen best-dresses. Light in the hearts of the mothers as they watch their sons at prayer, vying with the elders in their swaying devotions.

No matter that the King David Hotel sign is rusty and broken, that the hotel carpet is worn, that the flock wallpaper has faded from deep burgundy to pale rose, that the coffee cups are cheap and chipped, that the cakes they munch are just a little stale, that the waiters who move among them are threadbare, stained and spectral. For this is the first night of Chanucah, the Festival of Light. Chanucah, when the God of the Israelites performed a great miracle for His people. Chanucah, when the Maccabees smote the hordes of Antiochus and drove them from the Temple. When the corruption of Hellenism was finally driven from the soul of Israel.

A closer look at those spectral waiters reveals three who are more substantial than the others. A short, thick-necked man with a bull of a body wearing tails and immaculate bow-tie. A thin blond man in his early twenties, sad blue eyes. A tall, straight-backed man with crisply starched white jacket and fierce, red hair.

CHAPTER 5
Bournemouth, 22nd December 1965

Walter had never known real terror before, real throat-parching, gut-wrenching terror. But in that slow-motion instant as he watches water being thrown from behind him into the flaming chip pan, he knows for the briefest of moments what their suffering had meant.

Pure instinct makes him cover his face with his hands. No pain at first, not even intense heat. That came later. Then someone lays him on the floor, cuts the jacket and shirt from his body, bundles him towards the huge hotel sink, and plunges his arms and face into cold water. He hears someone call, 'Ice! Ice!' A few seconds later there are screams, terrible screams, they do not sound like him, they do not seem to come from him, but he knows somehow that it is him.

He hears a voice he does not recognise, intense, reassuring.

"Listen to me very carefully. You are in terrible pain now, but it will pass. I promise you it will pass. It will stop very soon. You will be alright. Do you understand? Just a little injection and the pain will disappear. Then Walter feels the needle slide into his sub-clavian vein.

* * *

A young man is sitting by his bed when he wakes up in the crowded hospital ward. Someone he vaguely recognises but cannot place. Of course, it is Michael, the new boy. Student, commie-waiter, intense, serious. Hardly typical of the staff at the King David. He remembers the day Michael had arrived in reception, looking like a guest who had stumbled into the wrong hotel. When was that? Yes, it was two days ago. Friday evening. He thought at the time that there had to be a mistake. A blond youth with no head covering, smoking on the eve of the Sabbath, strolling into reception asking for Reuben, the head waiter. He'd have never been given a job if they hadn't been so short staffed. But in a few hours they would all have to go scurrying around with cakes and tea while the candles were lit and the songs were sung.

Well, they had one thing in common at least. They both kept themselves to themselves. Hadn't spoken a single word to one another. Michael leans forward.

"How are you feeling now?"

Walter recognises the voice. It still has the same reassuring quality.

"Better."

Michael smiles.

"I told you that the pain would stop."

Walter has not seen him smile before. He seemed to be living in some troubling day-dream, wouldn't make many tips from the customers with a face like that.

"So it was you who...?"

"Of course, no-one else had any idea what to do. Astonishing how little people know. A kitchen can be a very dangerous place, especially a hotel kitchen."

Bournemouth, 22nd December 1965

Michael examines the backs of Walter's hands taking care not to touch them.

"You were lucky, very lucky, mainly second degree burns. Nothing too serious. They will let you out tomorrow."

"Thanks to you, sir."

Michael extends his hand in an air handshake.

"Turner. Michael Turner."

Walter does the same.

"Willy Krillink."

They smile wanly.

Michael takes a camera out of his pocket.

"Look, Willy, I'm still really a student. This is my first real case, you know, helping you. Would you be very offended if I took a photograph of your burns? I would like to keep a record of this case."

Walter tries to hide the horror.

"Well, I..."

Michael backs off instantly.

"No, no, I do understand. Too intrusive. I fully understand. Just forget it."

He stands up and moves to the door.

"Just looked in to see how you were. Better get going. Don't want old Reuben on my back."

Walter just manages a brief, "Goodbye sir," before Michael turns and leaves.

CHAPTER 6
Bournemouth, 28th December 1965

The faded hotel dining room on a miserable, wet Tuesday. Lunch has finished. It is time to prepare for the ceremony of the lights again. Walter is piling the heavy, saggy-seated, gilt chairs onto the round tables so that he can hoover the floor without stopping.

Michael has just finished cleaning the menorah, polishing it so vigorously that it is glowing fiercely in the light of the miserable wall lamps.

Reuben watches them both closely. He does not like these two *goyim*. The toffee-nosed blond boy and the straight-backed German who claims to be Swiss. Yes, just as he thought, Michael is getting it wrong again. The menorah has to be placed in the very centre of the grand piano. This idiot is going to scratch the woodwork if he tries to drag it into place.

"Lift it, lift it. Don't pull it!"

Michael tries and fails. He tries again, goes puce and gives up.

Reuben picks the huge menorah up as if it is a toy, tossing it from hand to hand. He hefts it onto his right shoulder and starts exercising with it as if he were weight-lifting, extending his arm vertically again and again. Four, five, six, seven times without any effort. Then he places it back on the centre of the table with the same hand.

"You know what we called people like you in Vilna in the old days, Michael? A *nebbish*, a shrimp. You need to do some real exercise, not that pansy running."

Walter stops his work and strides over to the menorah. Wordlessly, he picks it up in his right hand and performs the same lifts as Reuben, but this time he is lifting at a 45 degree angle and doing it at twice the speed.

"You should try it this way, Mr. Levy, sir. It is considerably more difficult."

Twelve, thirteen, fourteen, fifteen lifts without a flicker. Then he replaces it in the centre of the piano and goes back to his hoovering.

Reuben pales and leaves the room.

CHAPTER 7
Bournemouth 6th January 1966

The friendship between Walter and Michael does not develop quickly. For some time they nod to one another, like shy schoolboys. One afternoon Walter notices Michael in the locker room removing his waiter's uniform and putting on a singlet and running shoes.

"Do you like this running that you do, Michael?"

Michael doesn't even turn.

"Love it. Try to do it every day after lunch. Keeps me sane."

"Perhaps I will accompany you on an occasion?"

"OK, but I warn you Willy, I am very fit."

The next day Walter is waiting. He is in a new top of the range track suit and expensive running shoes. He lasts about thirty minutes and has to turn back. Michael had not spoken a word throughout the run. Just increased his pace on the inclines.

A week later, Walter is doing the whole distance. They run along the sea front, past mothers with fractious, shivering children, faces and arms rouged by the wind, exhausted by the steep climb from the beach. Past the art-deco hotels with their front porches and ancient card-playing guests. Past the seedier guest-houses, once proud, with their flaking stucco and cheap doors, beyond the edge of town where the road gives way to cliffs. They clamber over inhospitable dunes and rocks to find a narrow path which leads inland. To Michael's irritation, Walter is getting stronger than him, fitter despite the age difference.

Their conversations are guarded, neutral. The weather, the football, Reuben, other waiters, until Michael changes the rules.

"I don't pretend to like them. They are not an attractive race. The overweight women with their whining and their wigs. The unclean men with their beards and their endless babbling to their deity. The pushy, greedy children. They see themselves as 'The Chosen People' and the rest of us as inferior."

Walter says nothing. He simply runs faster.

* * *

The weeks pass. It is seven o'clock, Wednesday, their night off. Walter turns up with an Indian takeaway at the dank garage which Mrs Bowsher, Michael's landlady, insists on calling her 'annexe'. Michael has been studying. A copy of Grey's Anatomy is open on the bed. Walter flicks over some pages. Checks himself and stops.

"May I ask, how far have you progressed with your medical studies?"

"I'll get my first real job next March. Junior Registrar."

Walter hesitates for a split second and then hurriedly opens the food.

"I hope you like Indian food. This is my ...my staple diet in these days. Occasionally I also eat Chinese food."

They eat in virtual silence.

Takeaway food becomes a ritual. They never discuss it. Walter just arrives at the same time each Wednesday evening with a different selection, Chinese, Indian, Hamburgers, always too much for them to eat. Usually they play chess, but if there is a television

Bournemouth 6th January 1966

programme one of them wants to watch, Michael would struggle with his tiny set and the fractious aerial until he gets a half-decent picture. They favour news and documentaries, and talk about what they have seen.

They have almost finished their meal one evening when a news item comes up about the Animal Welfare Act in America.

Michael is incensed.

"How can they do that? How can they prevent us using animals to save human lives? That's ridiculous."

Walter seems embarrassed, unsure.

"Well, at the very least, do you not agree that the suffering of all creatures must be minimised."

"Of course, but this will stop so many good experiments. The Americans are so hypocritical. They regularly do research on terminal patients and criminals. They see nothing wrong with that, and neither do I."

Walter pales.

"How is it possible for you to articulate that thought? What happened to your Hippocratic Oath?"

"Look Willy, my job is... will be, to save lives, right?"

"Of course, but to save lives, not to take them."

"Any minute now you're going to tell me that the Americans shouldn't be making use of the experiments the Nazis did even though they have already saved a number of their pilots by using them."

Walter is silent for a long time. He looks at Michael with a mixture of disbelief and suspicion. Then he makes a decision.

"Very well Michael, we will have a formal debate on this matter. The subject of medical ethics. First, any medically trained person who uses this information, the results of experiments like this, who profits by it in any way, is an accomplice to the greatest crime in history. A crime which has already turned the German nation into worse pariahs than the Jews they tried to destroy. They will have to live with that for generations, probably forever."

"The genocide, yes of course, Willy, but if we use the results of medical experiments after the war, it doesn't mean that we committed these crimes. The fact is, knowledge can't be unlearned. The genie can't be put back in the bottle."

"But may I ask how is it possible to trust this so-called scientific information, Michael? Experiments performed by criminals on humans cannot be tested or verified. Even if papers were written at the time. They cannot be validated or duplicated."

"The Americans have tested them. They know that they work. Their Air Force is using the data. Anyway, 1966 is not 1944. There's so much more that can be done these days using pigs or chimpanzees. If the bleeding hearts authorities would allow us to, we could always find out. These people, the subjects of these experiments are dead. They no longer exist. How is saving lives going to hurt them? It's over for them. Are you suggesting that they should have died in vain?"

Walter is standing now, his knuckles white, the nails biting into the palms of his hands.

"Michael, can you accept the possibility that there is something after death?"

Michael smiles benignly. Walter's face grows dark.

"Please do not mock me Michael, scientists have been proved wrong before. The souls of these people will be in hell if their torture and death is exploited. They will be condemned, just as much as those who perpetrated these deeds."

"So what do we do Willy? Just ignore the data and let innocent people die. Surely we will be honouring the victims by using this knowledge. You can't bring the dead back."

Walter gathers up his coat.

"You are young. So young. You know nothing of life, of suffering, of pain. You cannot simply ignore those who suffered or their families. If any of them survived, they are already in torment. They would be tormented even more if they somehow received information to the effect that these experiments had been exploited, that the people who performed them actually made money from their obscene acts. And even if their death is final, don't their relatives have a right to feel that an injustice has been recognised, atoned for in some way? How can it be right for anyone to profit from such obscenity? From such total regard for human life, for human dignity?"

Walter's face turns green, he clutches his left arm, his forehead moistens, his eyes fill with tears. He turns his head away and leaves. Michael waits until he has been gone for some time, then he goes into Mrs Bowsher's house to make a phone call.

* * *

Walter's ability to insulate himself from the past had been perfect. He had felt nothing, until that discussion. How stupid of him to believe that he was safe, that he could ever be safe.

The nightmare is familiar to him. A youngish man, slight fuzz of beard on his face, emaciated but quite good-looking, sits quietly

Toxic Distortions

in the pressure chamber wearing a harness, impervious, resigned. The machine is turned on.

Then slowly, almost imperceptibly, a series of reactions begin to occur. The mouth first, teeth bared as the lips achieve high lability, then the cheeks hollow, the nose flares, the face is masklike, almost African in its horror. Then the secondary symptoms. Hypertension, palpitations. His face begins to go grey-green. He perspires abnormally. His pulse becomes irregular, it no longer corresponds with his heart. It has begun. Angina pectoris. Atrial fibrillation. Myocardial infarction. Death. The experiment stops. The face is benign, tranquil. The mouth opens and speaks.

"*Yahweh* will split your heart into a thousand pieces. *Adonai* will infect your mind with pain ten million times worse than the pain that I have suffered."

The corpse disintegrates in quiet, confident, laughter.

Walter sleeps on through the screams, the wailing, the dogs, the shouting, the sirens, the machine guns, the barred, blurred faces, vivid in their greyness.

But what happens next is worse, much worse. Walter begins to see the people he had tortured and murdered. They are sitting in the hotel dining room, waiting to be served.

"Walter, where is my chicken soup?"

"Walter, I have been waiting fifteen minutes for my lokshen pudding!"

They get up and shuffle, shaven-headed through the lobby in clogs and stripes, they hold their hands out to him.

"Help me Walter, help me, please."

Only Michael notices the pallor, the mumbling, the stoop, the sudden starts, the haunted eyes.

CHAPTER 8
Bournemouth, 12th January 1966

Breakfast was always such a frantic time. The whole dining room would fill up at once, immediately before morning prayers, everyone shouting for their French Toast, Orange Juice and Coffee. You had to be so careful in that tiny, claustrophobic kitchen. There were always far too many people in there, jostling with one another for orders, and the chef was always in a terrible mood at that time of day.

Walter doesn't even notice when someone jogs his elbow and the tiny pewter milk jug he is holding leaves a sliver of milk on Reuben's immaculate dinner jacket.

Reuben goes berserk. He is literally dancing with rage,

"*Raus! Raus*! You arse-hole Nazi bastard. I want you out of this building in ten minutes. Ten minutes, do you hear!"

Michael moves between them.

"Mr Levy, I know he didn't mean it. Someone knocked his arm. It wasn't his fault, I promise. I think it was probably me. I'll leave instead."

Reuben is adamant.

"What? I should let him off? Let him off. Just like that?"

Michael stands his ground.

"Let him stay. I will go. It was my fault."

"No! He must go. Now. At once."

Michael falters and then speaks out again.

"OK, Mr Levy, you need this thing to be resolved. That's obvious. Wait. I have an idea. The menorah! Of course, the menorah. You are both supremely fit for your age. Why not settle this by a trial of strength. Lifting the menorah from your shoulder like you both did the other day in the dining room. If Willy loses we will both go."

Reuben is quiet. The prospect of humiliating this German is too tempting. He nods his head.

"Tonight, late tonight, eleven, when everyone is in their room. We will do it Willy's way, the difficult way, at an angle of 45 degrees. Michael, you will count the number of times we lift. Willy, take the rest of the day off, do some training, you will need it."

* * *

The dining room is surreal, cavernous. Venetian chandeliers cast a rusty glow over the crumb-strewn carpet and scruffy table cloths, the nervous tie-less waiters, smudged chefs and kitchen porters, muttering, making bets, exploding softly with nervous anticipation.

The eight-branched candelabrum, the menorah, a massive presence, seems bigger than ever, dwarfing the chipped grand piano which nobody plays.

Reuben is already there waiting. Stripped to the waist, his upper body seems impregnable, robotic in its strength.

Michael arrives. He has brought pen and paper. He will mark every lift separately so there can be no dispute about the result. They wait. Reuben is sure there will be no competition.

Bournemouth, 12th January 1966

"So Michael, your German, where is he? What could have happened to him? Missed the bus did he?"

Walter comes into the room in his track suit. He has been running. He looks exhausted. He strips off his top and stands to face Reuben.

They spin a coin. Reuben wins and chooses to go first. He plants his feet like a weight-lifter and takes three huge breaths. Two of the stronger kitchen porters pick up the menorah and hoist it onto Reuben's tensed right arm. He lifts the candelabra up from his shoulder twenty six times at an even pace. Michael notes every lift carefully. Lift number twenty seven comes slowly and painfully. At twenty eight Reuben's face goes puce and his eyes bulge. Then his whole upper body becomes suffused with blood. At thirty lifts his shoulders sag forward. Half-way through thirty-one he staggers and his arm drops to his side. The porters just manage to catch the menorah before it falls to the ground.

Walter reaches twenty five lifts with ease. Even the next three lifts are no real trouble.

Then slowly, almost imperceptibly, a series of reactions begin to occur. The mouth first, teeth bared as the lips achieve high lability, then the cheeks hollow, the nose flares, the face is mask-like, almost African in its horror. Then the secondary symptoms. Radiating pain in his lower left arm, hypertension, palpitations. His face begins to go grey-green, he perspires abnormally. He recognizes the symptoms at once. His pulse has become irregular. It no longer corresponds with his heart. Angina pectoris. Atrial fibrillation. Myocardial infarction. But Walter does not stop lifting. He is laughing now, laughing and crying, standing stiffly to attention, raising and lowering his right arm, mouthing something with each lift. The words grow louder,

"*Mein letzte versuch. Mein letztes Experiment. Sieg Heil! Sieg Heil! Sieg Heil!*"

And then he falls. The menorah shatters around him.

* * *

Michael puts a pillow under Walter's's head and sends everyone away. Walter's face is bilious green. His breath laboured. He holds his chest and groans. In ten minutes this man will die. Michael's plan worked to perfection. Beyond his wildest dreams. This man was responsible for the death of hundreds of Jews. This man monitored their final agonies. This man looked without mercy on their anguish. This man will die, and his death will not be at Michael's hand. He will have killed himself. And yes, he will perish knowing that the one person he trusted, refused to save him. This man...this man...

"Michael, please help me! Please!"

Walter is screaming now, hands clawing out towards Michael.

...this man, this human being. Michael's resolve begins to waver.

The injection works very quickly, a slight colour returns to Walter's face. The ambulance arrives.

CHAPTER 9
Bournemouth 13th January 1966

The ward is full of male patients, most of them old, all of them in terror. The sounds come first, the coughing, the retching, the wheezing, the spluttering, the muttering, the whining, the whimpering, the moaning, the sobbing, the crying, the screaming.

The smell is breath-taking. Faeces, urine, vomit, disinfectant. The sweet smell of death. All pervading.

A lone, frantic nurse tries to cope with them, twenty of them. A word whispered, a bedpan changed, a drip replaced.

Even Michael, who is used to this, recoils at the familiarity, the proximity of the dying.

Walter is propped up on three pillows. His eyes, vast, purple shadows, his exposed legs distorted, swollen into huge, red tree-trunks. Someone has forgotten to replace the blanket. He gasps as he sees Michael, a tear trickles down his face.

Michael covers Walter's legs and sits by the bed. Walter's hand flutters out to him and he takes it. Walter starts to sob.

"So now you know Michael, you know who I am. You know what I did."

Michael's voice is flat.

"Yes Willy I know."

Walter smiles grimly through his tears.

"How long have I got?"

Michael listens to the ruptured castanets of Walter's breathing, and checks his erratic pulse.

"You are a good enough doctor to decide that for yourself, Willy. Do you want a priest?"

Walter's voice is harsh.

"I do not need forgiveness from some non-existent God. I need to stop this nightmare...this terrible nightmare. Always the same... the same. Every time I start to lose consciousness, he is there."

"Who Willy? Who is there?"

"One of my...one of the subjects...the pressure experiments. I know his words by heart now. He rises up and intones a prayer. He curses me...curses me."

Walter is sobbing.

"It is worse than anything else...much worse. Tell me what to do Michael, please. What can I do?"

"This dream is the embodiment of your guilt, Willy. It will always be with you. Unless...unless you can make peace with yourself."

Walter is straining forward now.

"Peace with myself. Of course. The easy answer. But how... how is it possible?"

"You must make a complete confession. Tell everything."

The relief in Walter's voice is palpable.

"Yes, yes a confession. I will tell you. Tell you everything."

A dim light is glowing in Walter's tortured eyes. His head turns away. There is a long pause. Michael's voice is low, soothing.

"Tell me about the early days, your first years of study, what were your motives then?"

"I wanted to cure people, to save them from suffering. Like you. Just like you."

"So how did you come to betray your profession?"

Walter is animated now.

"I have asked myself a million times. Every night. Every morning I question myself. I have no answers. No answers. The corruption happened while I was still at medical school. You have no idea what it was like in Germany then. A sort of national madness. A collective insanity. My father was a doctor. He had been badly wounded in the first world war and his pension became valueless so quickly. My mother saved us. She was a pharmacist, a good one. We all believed that National Socialism was the only answer, the only way to make Germany whole again, to bring back our pride, our national identity.

"It all seemed so logical Michael, so simple. The SS came to talk to us at college. I remember the lecture theatre that morning. It was full. No-one could afford to be absent, not when senior SS people were coming to speak. Some of the students did get very nervous, one of them went very pale and left the room before they had finished. But most of us were transfixed.

"They spoke to us for an hour. They didn't cajole or coax us. They simply gave us the facts. We were, after all, trained scientists. The Romans had used the results of medical experiments on slaves to treat their wounded legionnaires. For the first time in two thousand years we would have that opportunity. A chance to conduct experiments on *homo sapiens*. Not mice, or guinea pigs or rats, or even apes, but humans. Similar to rats in many ways, but their physiology was the same as man, even if their souls were damned. My friend Sterberbett and I were the only ones to accept, the others preferred to use their skills at the front, repairing the bodies of our brave compatriots in the Wehrmacht."

"And that was enough for you?"

"No it was not enough for me. It was only part of the story. There was this new science, eugenics. We all believed it, all of us. We knew that many eminent British figures advocated it, people like Bernard Shaw and H.G. Wells. It was very seductive. But in Germany it was different. In Germany the Aryans were at the pinnacle of civilisation."

"And the Jews?"

"The Jews. Ah the Jews, Michael. You yourself have told me how you feel about them. For us they were the diabolical race. A race condemned by their own greed, their own preoccupation with money. A race which put money before morality. A race which thrived by sucking the life-blood from the Fatherland."

Michael speaks softly.

"Tell me about Dachau."

"Dachau..."

Walter pauses. His eyes cloud.

"Dachau was a universe turned upside down, a monstrous world in which all I had learned had to be unlearned. But we were the *Ubermenschen*. The Jews, they were worse than animals. Skeletal, filthy, ready to die. No, not ready to die, expecting to die. If not today, then tomorrow. What did it matter to them? Their God, their *Yahweh*, was waiting for them. He had called them to him. That's what I really believed."

"And these experiments? Your experiments?"

"Please believe me Michael, I only used people who were already on the point of death and I never did any work unless it had relevance to the war effort. I wasn't interested in working with sterilization or twins. No, this was important work. We were saving lives, helping the Luftwaffe. You are a scientist, you will understand. Our objective was to find out how to save our pilots if they were forced to bail out into freezing seas or pushed by a dogfight up to high altitudes. We would put our subjects into low-pressure chambers which simulated altitudes as high as 68,000 feet. Then we would monitor their physiological response as they died. We took cine film, photographs, recorded vital signs every few minutes. Pulse rate, ECG. We even dissected the subject's brains while they were still alive. It was fascinating."

Walter is animated now.

"Do you know we were able to prove that high-altitude sickness resulted from the formation of tiny air bubbles in the blood vessels of the pre-frontal cortex."

Michael leans forward.

"Did any of your subjects, survive?"

Walter pauses. Why is Michael asking this question?

"No Michael, no-one survived."

There is a long silence. Walter seems to have lapsed into a reverie. He sighs, then becomes focused again. Michael waits until he is fully aware.

"There were also experiments with toxins Willy, were you ever involved in them? Do you know anything about them?"

"The toxins. That was Sterberbett, he worked with the Pharmaceutical companies. Very great profit for him. He may even have published some papers on the subject."

Michael hides his anger.

"Why did you leave Dachau?"

"A number of us saw the writing on the wall after we were defeated at Stalingrad in 43. I resigned my post in 44 and joined the regular army on the Russian front. I changed my name of course. There would be records of the doctors who had worked at Dachau. We Germans always were obsessive about record-keeping.

"Those last 14 months helped me forget. I was working a 23 hour day, trying to save young boys and old men. Doing what I had been trained to do. Setting fractures, staunching appalling wounds, amputating gangrenous limbs, putting the worst cases to sleep with a kind word. That's where I began to recover my sanity."

"And after the war?"

"After the war Michael, I disguised myself as a civilian and managed to get to the American zone. I started practicing medicine again. I was more needed than ever. But the past would not release me. I would be standing on a station platform and the words, 'Achtung! Achtung!' from the speakers would transport me back to that other world. I gave myself up to the Americans, confessed everything. They sentenced me to ten years. I was released after five years in a disgusting prison."

"What did you do then?"

"I returned to work at the hospital. Some of my colleagues suspected what I had done. However, there were no condemnations. They realised that the madness could have infected them just as easily as someone else."

"Do you know what happened to Sterberbett, your colleague from medical school?"

Walter's eyes narrow. Why is he being asked about Sterberbett?

"He is dead, he was cremated recently."

Michael pauses. He has come too near to revealing his hand. Time to change the subject.

"But then you came to England to work in a Jewish hotel."

Walter has prepared carefully for this question.

"I received a phone call, Michael. A call late at night telling me that I would receive 'further information in the post'. Four days later a letter arrived for me. An American company name. I can remember exactly what it said.

"They were aware of the valuable experiments which I had undertaken during the war and believed that my work should be extended so that more lives could be saved. They offered me a position as head of a research facility in America. How could those monsters think that I was capable of profiting from what I had done? I did not reply, but if they had found me, others could do the same, so I left Germany as soon as I could and came here to England. That's when I accepted the position at the King David Hotel, a place where I knew I would be safe, serving the very people I had defiled, where I could expiate my sins."

"And could you expiate your sins?"

"For a while I seemed to forget. The guilt slipped slowly away. Until...until you. Until that discussion we had. The one about the experiments. For the first time in my life I really listened to the words I was using. Words I had never spoken before. I realised that I had not simply killed a few individuals for the sake of science and my country. I understood at last that I had sinned against humanity. Humanity. I saw for the first time that the relatives of these people, these subjects, could still be alive. Still suffering from that obscene injustice. That is when the nightmare, the curses, came back."

Michael leans in until his face is a few millimetres from Walter's.

"And that curse will come back again, Walter, again and again and again. It will haunt you even after death."

"Why? Why will it come back?"

"Because you have not told me the truth, Walter. Because you have lied to me. You did not use people who were on the point of death. You did not give yourself up. You did not go to 'a disgusting prison'. You did not go to prison at all. You did not come to England to escape the Americans who wanted to use your knowledge. You did not repent. You have not repented. And Franz Sterberbett is not dead. He is lying in his own clinic. He had a massive stroke as a result of your betrayal. You punished him because of what he did to your wife. Because of what he and Frieda did, because of their affair."

Walter tries to rise. He falls back exhausted.

"Frieda! My Frieda."

"Yes Walter, your Frieda. Or was she Franz's Frieda? Tell me about Frieda. Tell me about the journal she wrote when you were in Dachau, the crocodile skin journal. Tell me what she said!"

Walter's eyes grow wide with fear. His voice is almost inaudible.

"Walter, you called me Walter. *Wer sind Sie? Wer sind Sie?*"

"I am your nemesis Walter. That journal Frieda used. That journal belonged to my mother."

Walter stares wildly around him for a long time. His voice grows hoarse.

"It was you, everything was you. You sent me the journal. And here, the burning oil, the milk, the competition with Reuben. It was you, all you."

"Yes Walter, it was me. All of it. All of it."

"Your mother's journal. So you...you are a Jew!"

"Yes, Walter, I am a Jew."

Walter's breath is faster, his breathing more frantic. He struggles with the words.

"It is just as I feared all along. You Jews are the master race, and we Germans are nothing."

"We are not a race, Walter. We are a people. A people without a common ancestry. This eugenics you spoke of, this pseudo-science, is irrelevant. There is no genetic link between Jews. We are human beings. Human beings like you. Jewish wives betray Jewish husbands. Jewish children wet their beds. There are stupid Jews, lazy Jews, innocent Jews, guilty Jews, Jewish bigots, Jewish racists, Jewish sadists. Many Jews have lost their belief in their '*Yahweh*'. No, Walter, the only thing that binds us is the hatred the world has always shown us. We have been fashioned by you. Your loathing has created us. It will never destroy us."

Walter's voice is barely audible.

"There is a difference, Michael, a huge difference. No Jew would have done what I did. You would never have done what I did. Leave me now. Leave me and do not come back. Your work is done."

* * *

The stink, the squalor of the ward stays with Michael as he walks down the corridor. He passes a small, middle-aged man presenting a business card to one of the nurses. The man has fierce, piercing blue eyes. He is wearing a tan waistcoat, a green bow tie, a formal black jacket and pinstripe trousers. Quintessentially English.

CHAPTER 10
London, 25th March 1966

Narrow hall, serene in the early morning. Dull pastels seeping through fake Victorian glass. Door locked and chained. Barbour, umbrella, Hush Puppies and running shoes in their appointed places. The usual Guardian and a few letters litter the floor. He scoops up the letters and takes them to the kitchen table. Sad, grey envelope, English stamp. He opens the envelope with one precise incision and removes the letter. A small slip of paper, a key, a postcard, a short letter, lawyer's emblem. Bitter parody of the very letter which had caused him to embark on his journey.

Corrutherrs & Son
Solicitors at Law
The Chambers
Bournemouth, Hants

20th March 1966
Dear Dr. Michael Turner,
Re: Dr. Walter Borrelle, Deceased

Be advised that the firm of Corrutherrs & Son have been instructed to act as executors in the Estate of the *aforementioned Dr. Walter Borrelle who departed this earth on 4*th *January in the year 1967.*

Dr. Borrelle has bequeathed to you the enclosed details and the attached key. Please sign and return the Postcard to confirm that you are in receipt of the aforementioned enclosures.

Yours faithfully,
Corrutherrs & Son

The key is small, innocuous. A number is engraved on its side. The note is minimal. It contains the words

'Hikstrasse, 56, Zurich'

CHAPTER 11
Zurich, 3rd April 1966

The taxi driver knows the route well. He doesn't even bother to ask the number. Apparently everyone in Zurich knew that a foreigner, any foreigner, arriving at the airport and asking to be taken straight to Hikstrasse before even checking in to his hotel, would always want the same building, number 56.

56, Hikstrasse, nondescript, fading grey brown stone, windowless ground floor. Above that, rows of small, mealy mouthed, rectangular apertures made from darkly reflecting glass. Nothing to distinguish it from thousands of structures in this dull, grey-brown city with its clanging trams, impeccable, hygienic streets and well-dressed burgers. A single door appears abruptly, set diagonally into one side of the building. Asymmetrical, small, low, steel shod, embossed, studded with mediaeval emblems, portcullis-like, a bronze bell set in the centre, just above a rectangular observation window. He rings the bell. The window opens a few inches.

The distorted, distant, voice cuts through him, Swiss-German whine.

"*Schlussel bitte.*"

Michael holds the key up against the window and waits.

"*Funf Minuten, bitte.*"

He checks his watch and waits.

After exactly five minutes, the door clicks dully and opens a few centimetres. He moves forward and it swings in before him, closing silently as soon as he steps straight into the three-sided steel lift, no floor numbers, no alarm bell. Just a simple case of seamless metal, big enough for one person. The lift drops without warning. Unpainted, rough stone slabs rush up in front of him. Then he is in a different world, a world of impeccable Persian carpets, heavy, gilt-framed old masters, damask curtains covering *trompe-l'oeil* windows. Air-conditioning vents noisily drying the air, making his eyes sting, his throat constrict.

A middle-aged woman in a grey business suit stands there, hand outstretched, short black hair, face unexceptionable, implacable, emotionless. Michael hands her the key and she turns, wordless, her pace even, mechanical. The corridor is long, seemingly without doors, and opulent in its Versailles splendour. He walks behind her. No sound, but some slight variation in the atmosphere makes him turn slightly. Behind him walk two men, almost clones of the woman. Grey business suits, short hair, blank, hard faces. Their smooth, muscular movements, the only clue to their role.

A second small door, smooth, steel, glides open in response to some hidden command. He follows the woman in. The men enter after him. They stand either side of the inner door, arms loose by their sides.

He is in a brilliant, gleaming room. Large bronze table, polished to perfection. Walls of burnished metal. Floor to ceiling, identical, copper-plated, rectangular drawers, perfectly machined, almost beautiful in their completeness. Each blemished only by the two key-holes which stand three centimetres apart like microcosmic sentries. The woman produces a second key from a chain round her neck and approaches one of the drawers seemingly at random. She inserts the two keys, turns them simultaneously and slides the drawer half way out. It is longer and narrower than he expected. She signals to the men. They place it on the table. Michael moves towards it, but with the slightest of gestures she motions him to wait. The men remove a second drawer, then a third, then a fourth, then a fifth, placing each of them on the table before him. The woman hands Michael back his key and nods abruptly before the three of them turn and leave. The steel door slides and locks behind her.

He looks into the first box. He is expecting money, so at first it seems almost empty, then he looks more closely and sees them nestling in the corners. Diamonds, thousands of them. All sizes, all shapes, some huge amber emblems, others tiny, glittering masterpieces of fractured light. Two hundred, maybe three hundred stones.

The second and third boxes are more predictable. They are bursting with bundles of bank notes, numbered sequences, crisp, pristine. US dollars, Swiss Francs. The next drawer is full of papers, official papers and eight millimetre film cans. Reports of experiments, press cuttings. Photographs. A different Walter, a smiling Walter, standing there in smug oneness with his colleagues, holding a certificate.

The fourth box contains gold trinkets, necklaces, brooches, tiaras, cuff-links, tie-pins, childrens' charm bracelets, stars of David. Each more delicately wrought than the next. All of them radiant with grief in the harsh light.

The final box stands apart from the rest. He looks into it and clutches at the edge of the table to keep his balance. It is a full minute before he can bring himself to look again. His hands slip on the handle. It is crammed to the brim with gold teeth and fillings. Some still traced with black lines. The blood of his ancestors. And there is something else beneath the gold. A glint of black metal, ominous black metal. But no, it is not metal, as he carefully removes the teeth from around it he sees what it is. Alligator skin. The journal. More sinister than ever now, nestling in a world of terror, of pain.

POSTSCRIPT
London, 20*th* September 1966

Rain. Rain slanting relentlessly over the mourners, drumming insolently on the dented umbrellas, turning the earth to rivulets of viscous clay, dripping from the hats of the religious rent-a-crowd, shining the marble tributes, mingling with Michael's tears, rendering the rabbi's speech indistinct, blurring the edges of his prayers.

A sodden shroud slithers from the tall black stone. The rabbi closes his book, and intones the words. The damp, grey lettering.

"'In memory of Mathilde Rebecca Auslander who died on 15*th* September 1966 after a life of unutterable sorrow. She was a woman of extraordinary courage who saved her nephew by an act of supreme self-sacrifice during the Holocaust. Now, at last, may her tortured soul find peace.'"

Michael had wrestled with the wording. As he hears the rabbi's pretentious accent, the over-dramatised rendering, he hears no honouring, only awkwardness. Only hollow, disjointed phrases.

The rabbi turns to leave, guiding Michael firmly away. Michael shrugs him off and stands his ground. His voice hoarse with emotion.

"We are here today to honour the passing of my mother's younger sister Mathilde, who gave her beautiful young body to a filthy lout in order to save me from certain death in Dachau…"

There is a stirring, a murmuring among the mourners. The rabbi hisses his disapproval but Michael would not be moved.

"...She survived the deportations, the thousand indignities of concentration camp life, the starvation, the forced labour, the death marches and the torture of a debilitating illness. She was destroyed twice, once by the SS doctors' whose experiments condemned her to an agonising half-life. A second and final time by the defilement and corruption of the only thing she had left of her sister.

"Mathilde is only one of the many thousands who found the inner resources to fight back, to withstand the terror, the pain, the knowledge of certain death. In honouring her, we are honouring all those people.

"But there is someone else we must honour today. A woman from a totally different background, a gentile, a *petit bourgeois* who took me into her house, into her life, who nurtured me as her own. Every minute of every hour of the four years she sheltered me, she knew that she could be betrayed, arrested, tortured, shot, raped, gassed. That woman we must also honour today for her courage was as great as that of my aunt. And in honouring her I must also beg her forgiveness..."

Then he hears it, a pitiful keening, the sound he has not heard since that day in the Secret Garden, her anguish among the elegance.

* * *

Nothing. No sign of change. Only a faint hissing, a viper at bay. First, a weakness, a tiny movement, miniature bubbles of black lava. The bubbles grow and burst. The fire flares and flashes,

London, 20th September 1966

spewing dark smoke. Thick. Torpid. Pitch. Evil seeps from the cracks in the contorted black skin, whispers through the arthritic fingers of the Hawthorne, disappears in the misty branches of the ancient Silver Birch where he had sat with Mathilde a year ago. The hissing turns to a popping. The popping to a crackling. The crackling to a wailing. The wailing to a screaming. The journal is giving up its ghosts.

Crimson flames grow small and pale, flicker and fade. Flakes of burning, gold-fringed paper waver in their flight. Wicked ash shimmers, shrinks, subsides.

Delphine appears, somehow diminished. Michael goes to her and takes her hands. His grip firm, reassuring. His palms dry. She looks into his eyes. New eyes. She sees his forgiveness. His strength. Tears flow freely among the smiles, the embraces, the vanquishing of the past.

END

ACKNOWLEDGEMENTS

Survivors

The material for this work has been germinating for over ten years, but it was not until I heard Marcel Ladenheim's touching story in 2010 that I was inspired to write this novel. Even before meeting Marcel, I found myself drawn to the accounts of survivors. So many stories, so much suffering. Milton Einhorn, Koppel Kendal, (one of 'The Boys') Lalo Gatenio and his son Raphael. All these people helped me towards my goal by providing a sort of dream-like background to my level of awareness. Countless documentaries and books, both fact and fiction added to my sense of the terrible randomness, the total injustice of this obscene phenomenon.

Mentors and Advisors

Once I had embarked on the creative process, a number of crucial influences impacted on me: A chance meeting with Sir Martin Gilbert in which he confirmed my views about the venality of the Nazis by describing to me how Eichmann had asked for Argentinian currency in his negotiations with Kastner in the famous 'Jews for Trucks' deal. The help I received from the office of the Chief Rabbi of England in my attempt to understand the wording on Holocaust Memorials. The invaluable support and encouragement given to me by my friends - Cal McCrystal, long-term journalist and more recently book reviewer for such broadsheets as *The Independent on Sunday,* Professor David Frendo, a classicist with an acute mind, Peter Majer, Senior Lecturer in Drama and Performance studies at the University of Roehampton, Dr. Patric Choffrut, polymath, historian and linguist who checked my style as well as my attempts at French and German, Professor Paul Weindling, whose book *Nazi Medicine and the Nuremberg Trials* was a mine of information. Paul Kriwaczek, whose book *The Yiddish Civilization* helped me to understand the fiction that had pursued me throughout my life – the notion that the Jewish people were a race with pronounced characteristics. Howard Cooper and Paul Morrison, whose book *A Sense of Belonging* was a revelation. Pam Ruben, who was kind enough to give me an actual yellow star and the copy of Red-Cross letter from the camps. And finally, yes you guessed it. I must thank Lesley, my wife for putting up with my obsessive behaviour and slowly breaking down my entrenched views. Her gentleness turned this book into a far more accessible and balanced piece of work.

Teddy Goldstein, London 2011

ABOUT THE AUTHOR

After Oxford, Teddy Goldstein's fascination with the written word was never far from the surface. His career was largely spent in areas where he could express his creativity: Educational publishing, creating training materials, and scripting films. But it was not until later in his life that he really found his voice. At seventy, he took a series of courses at Birkbeck College and then went on to do a degree course in Creative Writing where he won a short story prize in the Middlesex University Literary Festival. As a result, he gained enough confidence to start 'writing through the skin.' It was then that he found himself returning again and again to a subject which had troubled him all his life. The random injustice of the Holocaust. The failure to punish so many who had murdered, not out of ideology, but from greed. The supreme irony of the fact that most of the Nazis killed Jews in order to steal, and not out of some fictitious desire to rid the world of the very race they had accused of venality.

BOOK CLUB DISCUSSION POINTS

THEME
How relevant are the themes of this book to the present day?
Is this novel a useful way of delivering information about the Holocaust?
Did you personally learn anything new about the Holocaust?
Did this new information change your view towards the Germans or the Jews?
Do you agree/disagree with the author's portrayal of:
   1) Medical experiments and medical ethics after the War?
   2) The idea that the Nazis put money before morality and killed Jews in order to steal?
   3) The contrasting natures of the post-Holocaust God?

PLOT
How quickly were you drawn into the story?
Which part of the story were you most affected by?
Did the story move at the right pace?
What did you think of the use of suspense?
Was the plot credible?
Do you think that Matron's predictions were justified?
Were you confused by the twists and turns of the story?
Did the sequence of events in Part Two seem natural to you?
What were your feelings at the end of the novel?

STRUCTURE & PERSPECTIVE

What was your attitude to the difference in style between Parts 1 and 2?

Did the structure of the book seem unnatural?

Should the final part of the book have been longer?

Do you feel that you can understand the attitude of the Nazi doctors more easily now that you have read the book and heard Walter's perspective?

CHARACTERISATION

Who was the strongest character in the novel?

Which of the characters changed as a result of what happens to them?

Are these changes realistic?

Do you feel that Mathilde would have been so devastated when she read the journal?

Do you feel that Michael's childhood and later neuroses were adequately described?

Were Michael's motives entirely unselfish? To what extent do you sympathise with him?

Was there a time when your attitude to him began to change?

Why was Mathilde so hostile to Delphine? How was this scene handled?

STYLE

Did you notice the absence of 'he said/she said' throughout the book?

Could you always follow who was speaking to whom?

How do you feel about the use of tenses in the novel?

What was your opinion of the descriptive passages?

Would you have preferred to learn more about what was going on in Michael's mind?

Part Two was written in a completely different style. Did this work for you?

RECENT PRESS REPORTS AND COMMENT

"A survivor of the concentration camps...has accused...Bayer AG of conspiring with the Nazis to conduct human medical experiments for profit." Source: BBC 1999

"...my deepest apology for what my country and I.G. Farben did." Helge Welheimer, director of Bayer's American Division. Source: Phillipp Minkes, Co-ordinator of 'Never Again' Cologne 1995

"The gigantic sum of almost 120 billion Reich marks, the equivalent of more than £415bn today, was taken from Jews in the form of special taxes and under arbitrary laws, before they were either forced to flee Germany or sent to the Death Camps" Source: The Independent Newspaper, 10 November 2010

Made in the USA
Charleston, SC
30 March 2011